RAVAGE

Fueled in FIRE

rebellion #2

WALL STREET JOURNAL & USA TODAY BESTSELLING AUTHOR

RYAN MICHELE

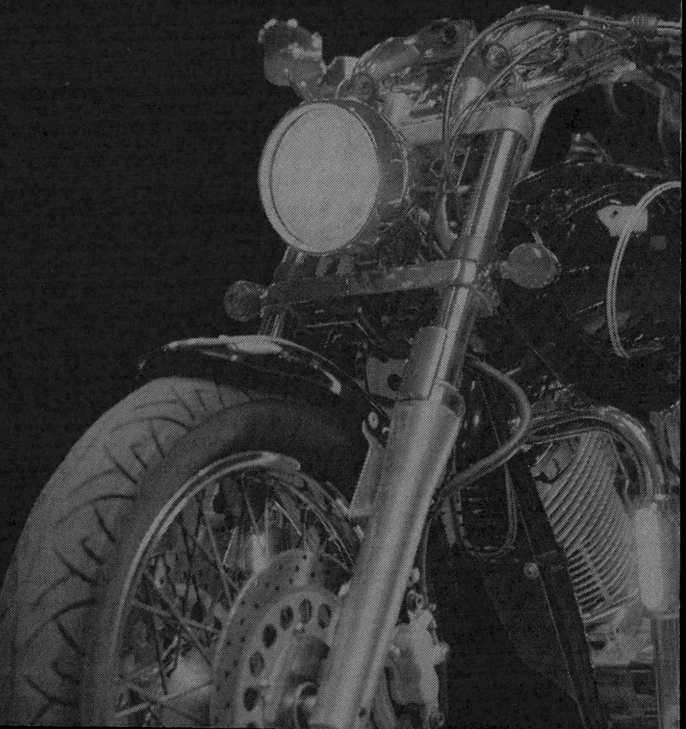

1st edition published: November 27, 2018

ASIN: B07K5ZLGBF

ISBN: 9781790188031

2nd edition published December 2022

IBSN: 978-1-951708-17-7

CONTENTS

RAVAAGE MC FAMILY TREE

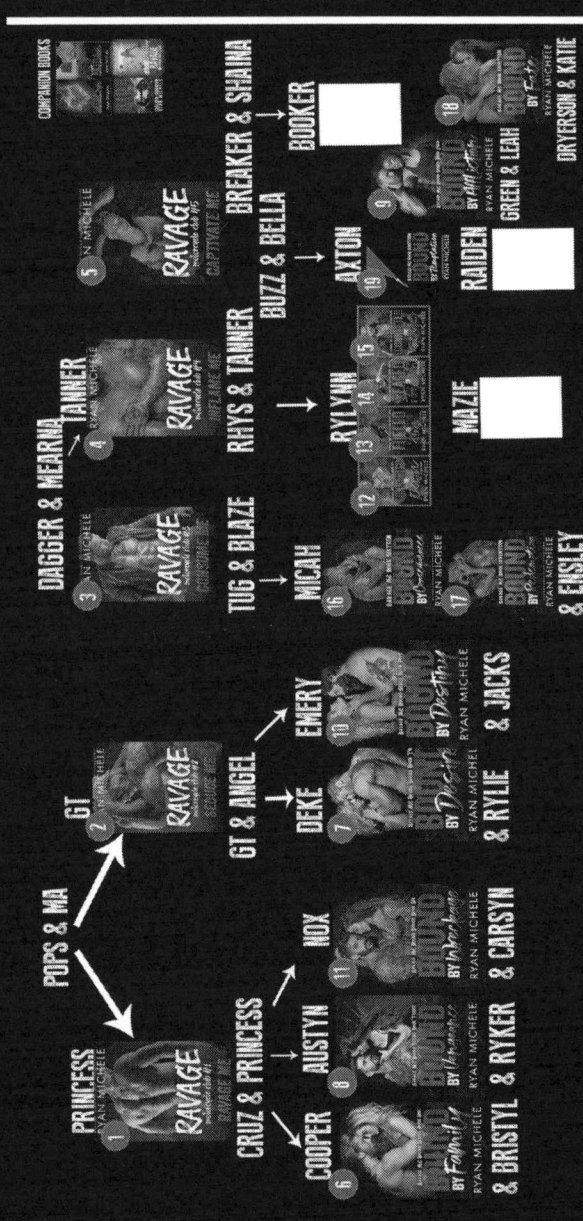

COMPANION BOOKS

POPS & MA

PRINCESS
RAVAGE ME

GT
RAVAGE — SEDUCE ME

DAGGER & MEARNA
RAVAGE — CONSUME ME

TANNER
RAVAGE — INFLAME ME

N MICHELE
RAVAGE — CAPTIVATE ME

BREAKER & SHAINA

BUZZ & BELLA

RHYS & TANNER

TUG & BLAZE

CRUZ & PRINCESS

GT & ANGEL

COOPER

AUSTYN

NOX

DEKE

EMERY

MICAH

AXTON

BOOKER

RAIDEN

RYLYNN

MAZIE

GREN & LEAH

DRYERSON & KATIE

& BRISTYL & RYKER

& CARSYN

& RYLIE & JACKS

& EINSLEY

BOUND BY Family
BOUND BY Indurance
BOUND BY Wreckage
BOUND BY Desire
BOUND BY Destiny
BOUND BY Innocence
BOUND BY Protection
BOUND BY Fate

RYAN MICHELE

BLURB

Rylynn

Ember to a flame, our pain started a passion fire that I couldn't burn out.

I wanted to be his light in the dark.

He needed me.

I would give him everything I had to give.

Crow

I had seen a lot in my life.

Felt even more.

Nothing touched this.

Every time I had something good, life had this way of taking it from me.

Could she be different?

Only with a passion burning so hot I didn't know if life would allow me to handle the flame.

We were connected in pain, *fueled in fire*, and we could only hope neither of us would come out of this... scorched and scarred.

We were Ravage MC.

Rebellion Chapter.

Ride free.

To my Dad
You've been my biggest cheerleader during this writing
journey.
Thank you for believing in me.
Love you.
Always and forever.
~M

CHAPTER ONE
Rylynn

THAT LOOK...

I knew it.

Felt it deep.

My heart broke for it on his gorgeous face. That look was what made me run and jump on the back of his bike. It was a pull, a calling to my soul. A connection.

Our connection.

Pain.

This strong, beautiful man was hurting.

He was broken in a way I'd only seen with death. Lost. Broken. The world falling around ones feet. The pleading in his eyes to me was something I couldn't ignore.

Snapping the helmet on, I took a chance and looked under the awning of the clubhouse seeing my father. Our eyes locked, and for just a minute I questioned what I was doing. His eyes were a mask of fury as he started to come our way, no doubt ready to pull me off this bike, but I wouldn't go with him.

I knew my father could tell this wasn't my first ride on the back of Crow's bike, only adding to his anger. My father could read me; hell, he could read anyone. The tick of his jaw, red face, and hands clenched were his signs of being livid. While my sister or I rarely got him to that point, I'd seen it directed at others.

I hated being the one to make him look that way. Loved my dad with everything inside of me, would do anything for him and that included taking his fury at some point in the future. Explanations would need to be made and questions answered, but right now, Crow needed me.

That simple fact trumped whatever I had to deal with later.

He had to know I'd be safe with Crow, being a brother and all, but he also knew my head was screwed on straight and no way would I put myself in any danger.

He may not know what was happening, but once I talked to him, and he got out his anger, he'd see.

Then he'd need to get over it because this was where I was supposed to be. I felt it down in my soul.

No matter what my family thought, this pull, this

pain I knew Crow was feeling, I wouldn't turn my back on him.

Couldn't. Crow needed me, and I needed him.

Luckily, Crow gunned the bike before my father could reach us. I wrapped my arms around Crow's middle and settled in as we took off through the clubhouse gate.

I didn't need to know what was wrong with Crow. I didn't need to know. I felt his pain and refused to deny the pull between us.

Whatever happened inside the clubhouse wasn't good for Crow because he looked on the verge of killing someone or crying. Neither of which gave me good feelings. It was his stricken face though that pulled me like a magnet. The pain and anguish was written all over him bleeding out and begging for release.

As soon as our eyes connected in the parking lot, I felt that pang of whatever was killing him on the inside hit me so deep, my heart cracked for him. He said nothing, but he didn't have to. His body told me everything I needed to know.

He was silently asking me to get on with him. His need for me burned so deep therefore leaving with him was the only option.

Plus, since the last time we spoke, I'd missed him like crazy and thought about him every damn day. Not that I'd given into every impulse I had to call him because clingy girlfriend I was not. It didn't change the fact that I couldn't shake him from my thoughts.

No one wanted to see someone they cared about hurt, and right now, Crow was feeling so much I didn't think he knew exactly what he was feeling. To me it felt like a kaleidoscope of emotions swirling around him, and there was nothing I could do but hold on to him as tight as I could.

The vibe coming off him was all encompassing and if my touch helped in any way, I was hopeful and thankful to give him that.

His brothers, Brewer and Wrong Way, rode alongside us, and I caught a few glances between them along with a shoulder shrug. Maybe they didn't know what happened inside, but like true brothers, they rode having Crow's back. It made me wonder if they knew if this was planned or not.

There wasn't a single word about Crow coming to Sumner that I'd heard about, and believe me—that would be something I'd remember.

Nor did I hear about the reason for the surprise visit. Hell, he had my number and didn't call me to tell me himself that he was on his way here. That was a question for later. Right now, this wasn't about me and I wouldn't make it that way by shoving my accusations in his face. That wasn't cool in the first place, so I locked it down tight. Me being here had everything to do with Crow and how I could help him not feel so lost.

The urge to comfort him was too strong to ignore, and my hand gave a little squeeze letting him know I was right where I wanted to be for him. It was a small gesture, but something pushed me to do it. That lost look on his face wasn't something I wanted to see ever again.

Since our last kiss, I missed him so damn much and nothing felt better than having his heat pressed against my front, feeling the tightness of his abs flex, and the wild beast below us. Hated we had to meet up like this, but thankful all the same.

Crow's hand came to mine on his stomach giving it a squeeze, lacing our fingers together, and holding it briefly there. That gesture made me feel damn good about my decision to get on his bike. He wanted me here with him. Wanted me to stand by him to get through to the other side.

There was nowhere else I'd rather be.

As I watched the road pass by us in a blur, we were heading in the direction of Alabama and had been on the road for a while. It was about a three and a half hour drive from Sumner to Rebellion.

I'd gone to the clubhouse to drop something off at the garage, therefore, when I hopped on his bike, I had nothing on me except the clothes on my back, the sunglasses covering my eyes, and the phone in my back pocket. I didn't want to let go of Crow to make sure it was still there either. Other than that, nothing. Not even a quarter in my pocket. But truly I didn't care. Crow needed me. No way I'd bitch or moan to go back and pack a bag. I'd figure it out as we went.

Dusk began to settle. The night was creeping in while the emotions still ran high. Crow flicked out his right hand, then turned off a ramp, pulling into a hotel. He cut the bike after parking and I jumped off, shaking my legs out then waited for him. My toes tingled like usual after a ride; it was a feeling that comforted my very soul. Watching Crow, his back rose and fell deep and long with his breathing. He was tense, and I had no clue what had happened.

His brothers parked their bikes next to us, each of them looking at me for some divine intervention, but I had none at this point. Being along for whatever this ride was with them.

Crow was slow to rise from the machine, but as soon as he did, he pulled me into his body, buried his head in my neck, and held me tight. I wrapped him up as close as I could, wanting to give him my strength to get through whatever this was. As the seconds ticked by and Crow hadn't moved, the worry got stronger. I wanted to absorb his pain.

My mind though, my concern, it was growing every second. Fuck, this was bad. Had to be because a strong man like Crow didn't get knocked down easily. It had to be a serious tick in his life to make that happen. I tried to mentally prepare myself for whatever Crow was going to throw at me because I needed to take on that heavy so he could release it. That I would gladly do for him.

"Brother?" Brewer asked, standing close, but Crow's body didn't move so he asked, "What's goin' on?"

Crow took deep breaths in and out as if calming himself. Only then did he lift from my neck standing tall, but had me tucked into his side, hand gripping on my shoulder. He was using me for stability, and fuck that felt damn good warming my soul. Strong men came in all different ways. Since my life was surrounded with them, I knew this was a big thing for him. Needing someone other than himself.

I felt honored he chose me.

Crow spoke, "Rylynn and I are gonna stay here for the night. You wanna stay or go home, that's up to you."

"What's goin' on?" Brewer asked again, this time getting closer. Wrong Way stood back, eyes glued on Crow.

Crow's arm got tighter, my hand going to his abs. We were a damn perfect fit.

"Need time. Nothin' for you to worry about, but I need shut-eye," Crow responded, but Brewer wasn't having it.

"If we need to prepare for something, we need to know," Brewer said, but Wrong Way surprisingly said nothing. He was doing that thing my father did. The 'searching your soul for your secrets' thing. Crow didn't recognize him doing it, but then again, I truly didn't think he cared at that moment. My man was at war in his mind.

I felt Crow's body go solid at my side. Angry waves started pulsing off him and making the confusion to take a hike in the blink of an eye. He was pissed and hurt, bleeding all over the ground, and Brewer was pushing. This didn't seem like a good combination at all. These were his brothers though. He trusted them so I needed to also, but much more. I was going to step in front of the path they were moving into to protect Crow. Even from himself. Hope bloomed that they would get it and back off.

Brewer saw Crow's change because I watched as his back straightened preparing for the reaction. He'd seen this side of his friend many times before and knew what was coming. Studying them both, they had a history. This was something to expect in an MC. It warmed my heart that Crow had brothers at his back who truly could read him.

"Nothin' to prepare for. Just need time." Crow bit out each word clipped and concise. I didn't look up at Crow, but judging from Brewer's face, Crow was menacing. I'd yet to see this side of him, but he was a man of mystery and knew it was somewhere in him.

He was Ravage after all. One couldn't be a brother in the MC and not have the balls to protect the ones around him. Sometimes, doing that got really dirty, but Ravage men always handled it. After talking to Nox about my grandfather and his retribution, while I knew, I didn't. That was a heavy weight to be on anyone's shoulders.

Wrong Way made a decision. He came up behind Brewer and slapped him on the shoulder, giving it a squeeze, obviously feeling the angry waves. "We'll stay here for the night. Let us know when you want to roll out and if you need anything," Wrong Way decreed and pulled Brewer with him into the hotel all the while Brewer said something low to Wrong Way. Brewer then kept looking behind to us not wanting to give up, but eventually, Wrong Way got him inside the door and he did.

Crow grabbed a few things from his saddlebag including a folder I remembered seeing him carry out of the clubhouse, and we followed behind as Wrong Way got three rooms from the clerk.

Crow was quiet and distant. Hell, if he could be on Mars it wouldn't be far enough for him at the moment. I didn't like the way it made me feel. Distance between us emotionally, mentally... I didn't know. I just knew the shit didn't sit right. His head was so far up in the clouds, I was happy he had the forthright to stop and get a place to sleep for the night. Bad shit happened when you weren't paying attention. Learned that lesson the hard way too.

Wrong Way handed Crow a keycard and told us the room number. On rote, Crow grabbed my hand, pulling me with him and not turning back. His brothers looked at me like I knew something they didn't, and I just shrugged my shoulders with a wide expression because I had no fucking clue what was happening. His brothers and I were on the same page here.

We all got on the elevator together and exited on the fourth floor. Crow pulled me to a door, slipped the keycard inside and opened it, pulling me through. Brewer and Wrong Way watched us go in and said not another word.

CHAPTER TWO

Rylynn

WHEN THE DOOR CLICKED SHUT, CROW RELEASED ME, shrugged off his cut, and removed the two guns he had holstered on him setting them on the table. He bent down and pulled off his boots. He gripped one of them tight as if he was going to chuck it across the room through the large picture window. But he held back, tossing it to the floor instead.

He sat on the bed with his head in his hands, elbows to knees looking down on the floor. Deciding to give him a moment, I went into the bathroom, shut the door, peed, washed my hands and tried to get my hair to calm down. It was amazing what wind could do to it. Even pulled back in a ponytail didn't help the rats nest it turned into. In reality, I was lucky it wasn't loose, but preferred it in a long braid while riding. Finger combing helped little, so I tossed it up in a messy bun. Whatever.

My phone, luckily still in my back pocket, had missed calls, but rather than give it my attention, I turned it off and set it by the sink with my sunglasses.

Coming out of the bathroom, Crow hadn't moved an inch. The rigidity of his frame and his unsteady breathing pulled at me like a noose wrapping tight around my neck, making the room almost stifling. He gave nothing away as how to help him.

Indecision hit me, but like I always did in life, I went for it sitting next to him, the mattress scrunching under our weight.

Lightly, I touched his back. He didn't move and we sat like that for a long time, not a single word, just that connection between us. Since I had no clue what was wrong, there was nothing for me to say. It was up to him, and he needed time. Therefore, I gave him that by releasing him then bending down and taking off my boots and socks, running my feet over the carpet. Sock fuzzies were the worst.

This act must've got through to Crow, because he fell to his back on the bed, arms extended up, looking up at the popcorn ceiling. I never understood why people did that finish to ceilings. My grandma's house had them on the ceilings and walls. Many cuts and scrapes came from running into it over and over again through the years. My right elbow had a scar from when I hit really hard. It was also the moment my grandfather decided the popcorn needed to go and had a prospect scrape it all off and redo the walls.

I laid down next to him propped up on an elbow, peering down at him. He didn't meet my gaze; instead, he began talking to the ceiling.

"Found out today that the dad I thought I had for thirty-three years really isn't my father." His words were strained coming out, and he closed his eyes.

My breath caught at how big of a blow that could be to anyone's life. I felt devastated for him, and my heart seized.

I couldn't imagine my dad not being mine, just one day something pop up like this and change my life forever. That hurt—the betrayal, the confusion. It would be so deep and ingrained it would probably never be able to get cleaned out. And Crow was getting hit from it.

Damn.

I could only imagine how he felt. How over-whelming this had to be.

"My dad's been there through everything. Raised me on his own because my mom was, and still is, a flighty bitch. He was there for every practice, game, school event—everything. He's been my rock since I was brought into this earth and now..." He paused, and my heart broke for him. "Come to find out, he's not my biological dad."

We sat in silence for a moment. I wasn't sure how to bear the weight of his pain.

"He's mine, but he's not anymore." The words came out low and heavy.

My hand reached out touching his chest where his heart was beating over time as he laced his fingers with mine and continued. "I don't understand how all this happened," he said on a squeeze.

"Break it down for me, and I'll help. Puzzles are my thing." I was doing the only thing I knew how to do, get to the root of the problem and tackle it.

Instead of doing so, he looked over at me, wrapped his hand around my neck and pulled me down to him, our lips connecting immediately.

It wasn't long, but it was fantastic.

The kiss felt more of a need. A need for the connection we shared. A need for the comfort he desired. A need for his heart to stop bleeding, and I was the only one who could give him that.

He tucked me to his shoulder, my head resting there, our legs tangling as they hung off the bed. Crow was quiet once again, but his heart thudded in my ear. Steady and strong. It was a sound that brushed off the cold left there from the last time we parted ways.

After awhile he spoke again, and what he said next rocked my world. "Found out tonight that Cruz is my biological father."

It was my turn to go still as a rock. My limbs felt

like concrete, and every molecule of air around us froze in time. Crow was Cruz's son? How was that even possible? So many questions ran through my head wanting to fix this and find out the answers. I wanted to give comfort to the man beside me. Cruz was a good man, had a good family. This wasn't a bad thing even if it felt wrong right now. My mind wanted to put all the pieces together to create the complete picture.

First, I went with the obvious ones. Narrow down the pieces of this puzzle quickly and efficiently. "How do you know that? Did Cruz tell you? Did he have proof." Okay, so it was three, but all very pertinent to the situation. There had to be some kind of proof here. No way would Cruz just spring this on Crow without it. He just wasn't that kind of guy.

"Showed me DNA paperwork that says it's true. Pictures of him and my mom together around the time I was conceived." He nodded to a folder he tossed down with his bag. "It's all in there." His eyes glared at the paper like it was his enemy.

I guessed maybe it was since it turned his every memory upside down.

My itchy fingers wanted to reach for the information, but instead I asked, "Did he know this when you were born?" In my gut, I knew that answer though. Cruz would never have allowed a son of his to be taken out of his life. That there was no doubt. For some reason, I just needed to hear the answer. Part of me wanted to say it out loud to verify the man I knew Cruz to be, but in some way maybe so Crow could hear it too and realize he wasn't the only one shaken by this news.

"No, just found out." He paused.

"Okay, so how does he know for sure then?" The information he was giving me was good, but there were missing pieces to the puzzle.

"At thirteen, I went to juvie for theft. According to the dates on the paper, the sample was collected at that time."

I filled in, "And Cruz had it run with his..."

"Yep. Ninety-nine percent positive that I'm his oldest son."

"Holy shit." I breathed deeply against his chest. Cruz didn't fuck around when it came to his kids. He was a fantastic dad and a great club president to the Ravage MC. He was also straightforward. This all had to rattle him as much if not more than Crow.

Hell, I'd known Cruz all my life, and I didn't know how to process it all quite yet. Small steps. That was where I needed to take Crow for this journey.

"Where do I go from here?" Crow spoke, and his words were laced in a sadness that I ached to ease from him. "One, I don't know if my dad knows about this or if he's as clueless about my parentage as Cruz and I have been. I want to believe he didn't know for some reason that feels like it would hurt less. But then I think of him and hope that he did know so it doesn't come as a blow to him. I know I need to talk to him about it, but fuck if he doesn't know it'll crush him. He's already sick. I sure as hell don't want to add any pain, but need answers at the same time." He swiped his hands over his face as if it would wash away everything he'd learned that day. When that didn't work, he opened his eyes and looked so damn tired. This had torn him apart, and it was warring on his face.

My heart hurt for everyone involved. Knowing Cruz for so many years, one thing he wasn't was a liar. He told things exactly as they were without hesitation, just like Crow. Therefore, I knew that Cruz wouldn't have brought this to Crow unless he was one hundred percent sure it was correct information. More so, Cruz was a great father to his kids, and him not having that opportunity with Crow must be killing him right now. Add in Crow's dad in Rebellion and it was a cocktail of misery for all. I wondered too about my friends. Cooper, Nox, and Austyn were the kind of people who loved fiercely. Family was everything to all of us, and this would be something they would take to heart.

"I don't know how to feel." He said, "Everything inside me twists like a tornado spinning out of control, throwing everything I've ever known about my life out the window, and it's takin' everything inside of me to stay grounded." He clutched on to me tighter, making me feel like I was the one keeping him grounded at the moment. I appreciated that. Loved it was in my power to give.

It was my turn to get real.

"You feel how you feel, babe. You have every right to be angry, hurt, surprised, scared or any other feeling. You were just dealt a blow that came out of left field, never even knowing it was a possibility. That's hard on a man. And it's not some *you're a pussy* thing. It's a life thing. When one's world is turned on its axis, it's normal to feel every way imaginable, and you need to let those out and not keep them bottled up. Feelings you push down only come back as pain later and worse."

His hand moved methodically up and down my arm. I wasn't even sure he knew that he was doing it, but it felt nice. It was as if we were giving each other our strength.

"I need to ask my dad about this, but how do I bring it up? Then the ramifications for if he doesn't have a clue and what they entail. If he does know, I don't know how I should feel. Pissed that he didn't tell me or honored that he wanted me to be his son. The unknown doesn't sit well with me."

Damn he was so twisted, hurt, and confused. It hit me that there wasn't much I could do to fix this except be here for him and listen. Being one to solve things, it sucked this one didn't have a solution.

He continued, "Then my mother. She comes back

to Rebellion all the time, and my father loves the flighty twat, gives her money, and Christ knows what else. Did she lie to him about me? Did she tell him that he was the father, or was she honest with him and told him the truth? There are so many questions, and right now I have no answers."

I rose, maneuvering my body so my chin rested on his chest. Everything in his demeanor showed the confusion, hurt, and betrayal. He was a big man broken in a way he didn't know exactly how to make right. I hated that for him because the only thing in this situation he could do was get answers and learn to deal with those. It was like a death and finding your *new* normal again. His would never be the same.

That feeling still lived inside me like a breathing dragon. The emotions all building and ready to spew out in flames.

Time. He'd need time.

"Give yourself tonight to process. Tomorrow, you feel up to it, you go talk to him. If he's anything like you, you lay it out for him straight up because that would be what you'd want. Just rip it off like a Band-Aid. It may hurt him, but from the way you talk about him, he loves you and biology doesn't mean shit to him. No matter what, he's always going to be your dad. Nothing will change that. If you have Cruz in your life too, that will take some adjustment, but don't get ahead of yourself. Unfortunately, he's the only one who can answer your questions besides your mom."

His body went tight. He didn't like his mother, that was plain to see. It was a shame because Crow was a good man, and she missed out on that. She fucked up there, big time. Her loss.

"I'm not talkin' to that fuckin' bitch. She needs to stay far away from me." He paused and there was no doubt this was true, then continued, "Then there's the fact that I have another father thrown into the mix. Fuck, I have two brothers and a sister. How fucked is that?"

"Sounds like you should be on the Springer show."

His lip tipped a bit in the corner, and I was happy he had a small reprieve. "Everything is chaos right now."

"How can I help?"

Crow pulled me to his lips and kissed me hard, slow, and wet. My body came alive, hands exploring his chest until he pulled back. When he did, there was something softer in his demeanor. He appeared to be a slight bit calmer. He heaved in a couple of deep breaths, and his shoulders loosened just a bit.

"Fuckin' starved, babe. Need food."

That wasn't what I'd expected, and my arousal took a nose dive which was stupid considering the shit storm he was going through. It was selfish, and that wasn't in my personality. It made me feel like shit, and I pushed it all away putting my focus only on Crow. Whatever he just let go of was big. I'd need to feed him and get him sleep.

"Right. I'll see what they have that delivers around here."

He kissed me with a touch of his lips and whispered, "Thanks for hoppin' on the back of my bike, Pixie. Needed you here with me."

The feeling like shit faded as the warmth filled my chest. This man was torn in two and needed *me* here with him.

I swore in that moment a huge chunk of me fell in love with Crow.

We ordered Mexican and ate. Crow was quiet through this, and I didn't press not knowing how exactly he handled these things, learning this and giving him room.

The light from the television shone through the bare room. There was no sound only the flickering of the light illuminating the space and dancing on the walls.

Since he turned it on then put it on mute, I rolled with it. Growing up, I'd learned to roll with a lot of things. This was another one of those instances, taking my cues from Crow.

My thoughts went back to Cooper, Austyn, and Nox. Austyn would've called me if she knew anything, especially knowing about Crow and my connection.

Since she didn't, Cruz hadn't told them. Fuck, this was going to turn their worlds upside down too.

So much time just... gone.

Time was a thing to treasure. It was a golden item that once it was gone you'd never get it back.

Ever.

Princess, she'd be pissed at first wanting to kill Crow's mother, then she'd welcome Crow with open arms. That was the kind of woman she was. She loved fully and to the death for those she loved and cared about. From the stories told over the years, she did the same thing with Cooper. Even with thirty plus years passed, Crow would be no different to her.

How strange was it though that Cruz was the president in Sumner and Crow was the President in Rebellion? Two presidents of the same club, but different charters. That shit should be written in a book somewhere.

My mind was everywhere. It was with my Ravage family in Georgia, and it was with Crow. This was going to be a hard pill for everyone to swallow. The only thing I could do was give Crow enough water that he didn't choke as it went down. I would be his liquid, a safe place to fall.

"Thank you," he said quietly, my attention going to him instead of the muted TV.

"Nowhere else I'd rather be."

"Missed you." His words made the butterflies set off

in my stomach which hadn't happened before, ever. Fucking butterflies. Me. I was in trouble, falling deeper for this man with each tick of the clock.

"Missed you too," I said, maneuvering to look Crow in the eyes. The hurt was still there. Processing this was difficult for him as it would be for anyone. This strong man fighting within himself trying to make it through the other side.

He closed his blues and when he opened them once again, the fire and desire was burning bright. The pain was gone, and in its place was fire, passion.

His lips came to mine hard, deep, and rough. This wasn't a kiss of gratitude. This was a kiss of want and need. I took the invitation without hesitation, needing him just as much. He rolled pulling me under him, his weight feeling magnificent.

Our mouths danced creating a buildup of what was coming, driving our desire for one another. We were so in sync with our movements from our lips, bodies, and hands, every touch was countered. Our lips took from each other, but gave in the same respect. My body already alive began to burn, my skin hot, and breaths picking up speed.

His large hands skated up the sides of my body taking my shirt with it. One minute he was kissing me, the next my shirt flew away to the floor and his lips were back to mine. Luckily that was all I had on. His hot skin touched me; add in the kisses and my skin began to prickle.

Between my legs throbbed, wanting to be filled by this man. My mind was completely on board with that want.

Crow maneuvered pulling off his boxers, settling between my legs and pressing inside me inch by inch, his eyes never leaving mine. He rooted himself all the way in and stilled. My body conformed to his size, and I wiggled my hips to get a reaction.

"Need you to move," I breathily demanded.

He kissed me then ever so slowly began to thrust in and out. Each movement slower than the last. My body screamed, hands going to his ass to squeeze him to hopefully get him to move. I needed more friction, and as soon as it came I'd shoot off like a rocket. I was so close. Climbing higher and higher, I was right there.

His cock pressed all the way inside me and stilled once again.

"What are you doing?" I growled, getting seriously frustrated.

He brushed the hair away from my face and kissed my lips softly. "Come to Alabama with me."

"Thought that was what I was doing?"

"Good."

He kissed me deep once again, his thrusts becoming so hard the headboard kept banging against the wall. Over and over he pushed and pulled inside of me.

The orgasm hit me like a sledgehammer taking away every thought but just one.

Should I go to Alabama with him? Too late.

That decision was already made.

CHAPTER THREE

Crow

Loved having Rylynn on the back of my bike. Her arms were wound so tight around me it felt as if she was the one grounding me. Never found that in a woman before.

Women.

I had my share.

I was young and dumb. Pussy was pussy except with Sophia, and that was before I knew love and pain could mix into a concoction no voodoo priestess could top. I'd loved Sophia back in high school, but not once did I feel like she tethered me to the earth. Not like this. Not like Rylynn. She was everything holding me down. So very much that I wasn't sure she realized it yet.

Wrong Way and Brewer cut off continuing down the road as I turned us into the concrete drive of my house. Shutting down the engine, Rylynn climbed off and I did as well.

She stretched, her shirt going up and giving me a hint of her creamy skin. "Nice home you have here, Grizzly."

Wrapping my arm around her shoulder, I led her on the sidewalk to the house. "Yeah. Gotta have somewhere to crash. Can't do it at the club all the time."

Opening the door, she stopped just inside checking the place out while I tossed my keys on the small table. "Not much for decorating huh?"

"Nope. Comfort is all I give a shit about."

Rylynn pulled her phone out of her pocket and tossed it to the kitchen table along with her glasses. She was literally coming to Rebellion with nothing. I'd have to rectify that for her. She was giving me everything, and I would give it back tenfold and more.

Rylynn was mine. I took care of what was mine. Always.

Taking off my cut then sitting down to take off my boots, I made my way into the bathroom. After doing my business, I stared in the mirror at the man before me.

My eyes were as haggard as I felt.

The entire way here I went through questions, scenarios, and possible solutions to what my life had become in the course of a couple days. Each one different, and I really couldn't figure anything out until I talked to my dad.

The thing was, I wasn't ready to. As much as I needed to know, there was a huge part that didn't. It had nothing to do with the club and everything to do with my dad and me. The questions needed answers, and me putting it off did nothing but prolong the pain. The talk needed to be done. Luckily Goldie had Van so she wouldn't be there. Hell, my kids had other grandparents, uncles, and aunts. My head shook.

Coming out of the bathroom, I found myself grabbing my cut and putting my boots back on. Rylynn appeared stunned at my change, but covered it quickly. It made me want to go in the bedroom, tuck her under my blankets, and not leave for a week.

My gut was talking to me though, and it was telling me to go and talk to my dad.

"Sorry, Ry. Look, I've gotta go talk to my dad and get shit sorted. Anything you see here you're welcome to it. Take a shower, eat the food, dress in my clothes. Whatever. I'll be back when I can."

Moving to her, I planted a very fast kiss on her lips. I wished I had the time to show her my home, my life. I simply didn't. The past needed answers. Whatever the outcome it needed to be settled so I could move on and deal. I didn't need another problem and this current one was mammoth. There wouldn't be a solution overnight, but it would be a start. That was better than nothing, and at least I'd hear my dad's side of things.

"It's cool. Don't worry about me." She gave a soft smile, like she understood but didn't want me to leave her all in the same. The pull was so strong.

I pulled her closer into me. "For some reason, I just can't stop." She sucked in a sharp breath as I gave her a last kiss and left.

If I'd been in my right mind, I would've paid attention to how she looked standing in my door, shoulder to the frame, face a mask of concern. She cared. Deeply. She felt my hurt just as I did and was trying to be the strength I needed. Never in my life had a woman become my rock, someone I could depend on who gave a shit about me. Sure the cut got women, but that was nothing but cheap thrills that now didn't seem so great.

Rylynn though. She gave everything freely.

My feelings for her were growing by the second and put into hyper drive, but after my bike fired up I had to leave her in my home and deal with my reality.

Dad didn't live far, the drive nowhere near long enough to put everything in perspective, but neither was the trip here from Sumner.

My nerves were shooting all over the place, and it was a feeling a man like me didn't have often, if ever. All of this left me so confused and off kilter.

In the driveway was a red Mazda. Kara's car. Killing

the bike, I went up to the door, knocked twice then turned the handle. It opened with ease. No matter how many times I told the old man, he never locked the damn thing. He needed to.

"Dad?" I called in to see Kara on his lap riding him like the cowgirl she was. Fuck me, this wasn't the first time I'd walked in on them, but watching my dad get his piece never sat well.

"Son. Shit."

"Told ya to lock your damn door."

Kara smiled up showing off her tits and no doubt willing to do the both of us at the same time. That would never happen. Not only did I have sweet pussy waiting for me back at home, there were some lines there was no way in fuck I'd cross. "Get gone," I ordered to her, going into the kitchen, opening the fridge, and getting a beer. This wasn't a conversation that needed an audience. Hell, I didn't want to be in it, but deflecting would only make it worse.

Rustling came from the living room, and the front door opened then closed. My father came into the kitchen buttoning up his jeans. "What's goin' on, son?"

I took a pull from my beer. His answer mattered to me, and controlling my reactions was going to be difficult. "Got a call from Cruz. Wanted me to take a ride to Sumner."

My father went to the fridge and pulled out a beer of his own then motioned me into the living room. He didn't hesitate. He didn't freeze. Nothing in his demeanor said he had a clue about the bomb I was about to drop. Cruz calling me to Sumner didn't faze him in the least. He sat in his reclining chair while I sat on the couch and took another pull from my beer. Bourbon would be better.

"Do you have any idea why he would call me to Sumner?" Probing questions to him was a necessary evil because I needed to know if he knew the truth and hid it from me all these years. There was so much hope inside me that he didn't know. All the while that result would hurt him more. It made me a bastard of a son.

"Got some club business? Or that woman you bunkered down with when you had the run, she was from Sumner?" He took a pull from his beer then held it by the neck. His face didn't change. There was no strain to his features. Not even an extra blink to his eyes. No, he didn't know, or he was that settled into his lie that it had become his truth.

I tried a different tactic. "There wouldn't be any other reason?"

My father looked me straight on, not a flinch or even a hint that he knew what I was about to drop in his lap. "Just spit it out because I don't fuckin' know what you're ramblin' on about. But I can see it in your eyes, Crow. You got somethin' on your mind, give it to me."

Part of me felt relief, but I didn't know if I could

trust it yet. Was I just clinging to some strange hope and seeing shit that wasn't there? The other part of me hated the words that came pouring from my lips, knowing the anger my father would feel and not being able to cushion the blow because there was no way.

Rylynn was right. It had to be like a Band-Aid and see where we went from there. "Cruz says he's my biological dad."

My father bolted upright faster than I'd seen him move when I was younger. Red covered his face. "What the fuck did you just say?" Anger bounced off the walls. He didn't know. Had no fucking clue anything about it. His eyes were contained fury and pain. A pain I knew and had felt myself. While I was happy he didn't keep it from me, I hated that he had to know now. The ball was already rolling, and he deserved the truth.

"Cruz. Showed me DNA results."

He glared and crossed his arms over his chest, the same way he did when I got in trouble when I was younger, which was a lot. "How the fuck did he get your DNA?"

I shrugged, but gave him the answer Cruz gave me. I wasn't about to lie to him or sugarcoat any of this shit because I had too much respect for the man in front of me. "From the system. Remember when I stole that shit when I was like thirteen or so? They swabbed my mouth then, but fuck if I remembered it, but I intend to find out who it was. That shit was illegal as hell." The documents Cruz gave me didn't have a name on them, but did give a date which coincided with the theft.

My dad said nothing. So I continued.

"But you know the kind of man Cruz is. There would be no way in hell he'd come to me with this and not be one hundred percent sure it was completely true."

Anger bubbled in my father's eyes, and I couldn't take that hurt, rage, and confusion away. I felt it too. That slicing in the gut and heart that we never knew if it would heal or not.

"That fuckin' bitch," he growled, throwing the bottle of beer clean across the room where it crashed against the wall and shattered everywhere. "She told me you were mine. She'd come from the Sumner guys with another bitch. Fucked her and she ended up pregnant within a week. I should've thought about it, questioned it. I didn't. I fuckin' fell for that shit."

While it was stupid on his part, I was happy that he did. Who knew what my life would've been like if she hadn't left me with my dad and took me with her. He gave me the best life possible. He had to know that.

I rose and went over to my dad who stood by his old fireplace. "You pissed you had to deal with me?"

His face paled as he realized I was questioning where we stood now with the truth between us. "Fuck no. I don't give a flying fuck that we don't share DNA. I'm your father, end of story." I wrapped my arms around him giving him a hard pat of the back then stepping away. "That bitch though, she's gonna pay for this shit. She's been nothing but a pain in my ass since she walked into my life. Fuckin' loved that woman. Would've given her any damn thing she wanted. What does she do? Fuckin' pull a switch on me. Bitch."

"It's okay, Dad. Nothin's changin' between us. You gave me the best damn life I could've ever wanted. Gave me a family. You are always my dad, no matter what."

"Bet Cruz wants to get to know ya and all that shit." He moved around me and began pacing the room. He was going to make himself dizzy. Dammit.

"Yeah, but told him I needed time to process all of this. It's a bit much. And he's not pushin', Dad. He gets it. No worries there. He's not gonna show up tomorrow and get in my space. Need you to know, he's not takin' your place. I don't know what the fuck to do with all of this, but what I do know is you're my dad, end of story."

My father's fists were at his sides, arms locked up tight, face a mask of undiluted anger. He even started trembling. I quickly moved to him, getting in his space, hands on his arms. "Dad, calm down." Sweat trickled down his forehead. He grasped his chest, eyes flying to me in surprised shock as he collapsed to the ground in a heap. Kneeling beside him I tried to move his hand, but he wouldn't let me.

"What's going on?" I asked hurriedly, but I knew. The way he was grabbing his chest, the sweat, shortness of breath. He was having a heart attack. Reaching in my back pocket, I dialed 9-1-1.

"9-1-1, what's your emergency?"

"My father is having a heart attack. We're at seven-nine-six Rosewater Lane. Get here fast!"

I tossed the phone down then jumped up and ran to the bathroom looking for aspirin. Grabbing the bottle, I darted into the room, opened the bottle, and put a pill between his lips. "Chew this for me."

He tried, but his body was shaking, sweat coming from everywhere.

"Love..." he said, then his eyes closed and body went limp.

"No!" I screamed, checked for a pulse, didn't find one and started CPR. I'd never again bitch about learning this shit when I was younger. Press, Press, Press, Blow. "Come on, Dad!" Press, press, press, blow. "Breathe, dammit!"

It felt like hours, but could've been minutes before the paramedics came in the door.

"Move aside." I didn't want to leave him because I knew.

I just knew. There was no saving him. His body had given out.

He was gone, and it was my fault. I should've let it be and not went to him about it drudging up old shit. If I'd kept my mouth shut, he'd still be alive, here with me.

Pain was a tangible thing that decided to hit you from every angle imaginable, never relenting or giving up. I'd thought yesterday was bad, but it was nothing compared to this very moment with the paramedics working on my father, hoisting him on a gurney, and putting him in the back of the ambulance.

This couldn't be happening. My rock couldn't be gone.

The pain of betrayal cut deep, but not a damn thing in this world cut deeper than the loss of someone you loved.

It hurt worse.

CHAPTER FOUR
Rylynn

A KNOCK CAME TO THE DOOR, AND I LOOKED ridiculous. Crow's clothes made me feel like a child. They swam on me, but I needed a shower after the trip to get the road grime off me. I'd hand washed my bra and panties since they were all I had. They were in the bathroom and not on my body. Which wasn't good for whoever was at the door.

The knock came again, and I gripped the pants at the waist to make sure they stayed up. "In for a penny, in for a pound."

Unlocking the door, I swung it open. My breath caught in stunned silence as I took in the boy in front of me. Standing there was a clone of Crow, only younger and no tattoos. Sandy hair with blue eyes, same build. It was as if they put Crow in a machine and out popped this guy. It was uncanny.

"Who are you?" he asked, stepping into the house and looking around like he was meant to be there and I wasn't.

"I'm Rylynn. Who are you?"

He turned to me and I already knew the answer by his looks, but needed to hear him say it. It hit me hard, which I wasn't expecting. This guy couldn't be more than seventeen if that. Which meant, Crow had a child about the same age as me. It was a good thing age didn't matter to me or we'd be in trouble before we even got ahead.

"Greer. My dad here?" And boom—there it was. Confirmation. You'd think one of the times we'd spent together he would've told me that he had a kid. Maybe when we talked about my age, he would've thrown it out there that he had a son around my age.

Never a word about it though. This wasn't the time to contemplate these thoughts. There were bigger fishes to fry, therefore I locked it down.

Compartmentalize. My dad gave me this skill, and I found it useful in life. Tuck shit away, put the emotions at bay until it was time to let them loose.

"Nope. He went to his dad's house."

"Then why are *you* here?" He sounded agitated and not too happy I was in his father's space. His entire demeanor changed. It was strange because I could actually see it happen. One where he thought his dad was around, the next anger because he wasn't.

I closed the door, hearing it click and turned around. "Because he told me to be."

His eyes narrowed, and I could swear Crow was standing in front of me. All the times he'd gotten pissed at me flashed through my head like a blast from the past. Geeze. "Dad doesn't bring his *whores* home."

That struck me deep. The cut from those words was a wound I never wanted to obtain my entire life. The thought of being someone's whore. Their fuck toy. That was the reason I stayed away from the brothers, never wanting to become what I'd seen several times over and over.

I broke my own cardinal rule.

I made that promise to myself so that I would never be seen as this or feel like this.

Except with Crow, I didn't feel like a whore or club momma. I felt like a woman, a strong, fierce, sexy woman.

My expression stayed the same, not letting the pain of those words show. Everyone smelled fear and once they had a taste, they never let up until they got what they wanted and went in for the kill. Fear wasn't an emotion to share with others, never wanting them to get the upper hand on you. Never give anyone a tell on you or an inch of power on your emotions and control.

I was my father's daughter.

While this was Crow's kid and I should be patient with him considering I just popped up at his dad's house with no warning, I couldn't. There was no way in hell I'd allow him to talk to me like that. No way in hell I'd let anyone talk like that to me. Respect went two ways and at this moment, he had zero of mine.

I stepped closer getting into his space, but far enough away that he understood the words that came out of my mouth were serious. "One. I am not a whore. I know you've seen them around the clubhouse, but make no mistake, that is not me. You do *not* ever call me that again. Period. The consequences of it happening again will be on your shoulders. Two. You never disrespect someone you just met and have no idea who they are or what's going on the way you just did. Every word that comes out of your mouth you're responsible for. I don't give a fuck if you're what, seventeen?"

"Sixteen," he barked out.

"Fine, sixteen and think you're invincible in the world. You're not. You grew up in this life, and respect and loyalty run deep. I do not believe for one second that your father didn't teach you that."

His face turned to stone. "I respect those who deserve it. You don't. You're here for him to get his nut off and that's it. He never settles down with anyone the likes of you. So don't get your hopes up. And what are you? Sixteen too?"

"Nineteen actually and my father taught me how to be a good judge of character when it comes to people.

And, Greer, you're a shit one. All piss and vinegar. You want to be an asshole to me, fine, but don't expect me to take it because I won't. You want me to give you the benefit of the doubt, you earn that shit now."

"You act like you're going to be around more than a night. You're kidding yourself." He took a step back and crossed his arms over his chest.

I took one step forward, not giving him an inch. "And if I am going to be here tomorrow or the next? Don't think for one second I'll put up with your shit. You need to lock that down when it comes to me."

"Listen to you thinkin' you're all high and mighty. I could take you out," he snapped his fingers in the air, "like that."

To this, I laughed hard. While he was Crow's kid and I wouldn't put my hands on him, I would no doubt defend myself. This kid had no idea. "Right, and you're Einstein and know this for fact huh?" The kid was built, I'd give him that, but actual moves—I'd like to see him try me. Then again, Crow might have trained him and depending on if he were a good student or not, would either put me on my ass or not. Princess taught us all, especially her own kids, so maybe Crow gave his kid some skills. No matter what, I wouldn't back down. It wasn't who I was.

Because through and through, I was Ravage. We didn't back down.

I took in the young man in front of me. Every

fucking detail I committed to memory. Greer's fingernails were too clean. They didn't have the dust under them from a really good workout or working on an engine. He didn't have the air of an alpha in the making behind him. That didn't mean he wouldn't grow into it, but he just wasn't exuding power like most of the men in my life had even from a young age.

Something told me, he didn't live the life Crow did.

The door swung open, and I turned quickly hoping it was Crow so he could deal with his shit of a kid, but Wrong Way was there instead self-imposing in the doorway. "Get your shit," he ordered me, ignoring Greer. "Crow needs you at the hospital."

My heart slammed in my chest. I could feel it actually bouncing off the walls of my ribs. He couldn't be hurt. Just couldn't. "What happened?"

Wrong Way didn't hesitate. "His dad had a heart attack."

My heart sank. This was all too much, too fast, and too intense. I skirted out of the room grabbing my still damp undergarments and putting my jeans back on, then tying Crow's shirt so it didn't come down to my knees.

Greer could be heard in the other room talking to Wrong Way, then it was quiet. There was a small bit of hope he left. I wanted to deal with him on another day, not when someone could possibly die. His father's life was turned upside down and now before he could settle his own feelings this happened. For today, Greer got a pass from me.

Slipping on my boots, I made my way back into the living room, bent down, and started tying. "Is it bad?"

"Yeah. They took him in to try to revive him, but it doesn't look good," Wrong Way explained, not giving much away.

"Fuck."

"See you met one of the kids."

I finished tying and stood up grabbing my phone and sunglasses. "One? How many does the man have?" I fought and managed to keep my voice steady and not let my surprise be known.

"Two. The other is a girl. Ten-years-old."

Christ, that was how old Mazie was. I had to shake all of this off. "Let's go." There was no more to say. I climbed on the back of Wrong Way's bike, and we shot like a rocket as I clutched his sides. It didn't feel right being on this bike with him. I found myself letting go of him and maintaining my balance by gripping the seat. Wrong Way wasn't a bad guy, he just wasn't my guy and being on his bike wasn't my place.

Two kids. This proved I didn't know shit about Crow except for we were magnificent in bed. It was the connection though that had me keep coming back to him. This invisible thread that didn't want to release from him. There were so many things I didn't know about this man. Would this crazy pull be enough? Was this real? The more I let my mind wonder the more intense my emotions became.

True, he told me about his mother, father, Cruz and I knew somewhat about his club, but had no clue what his favorite food was or his favorite football team, kids. Maybe coming here was a stupid idea. Maybe the pain of losing my grandpa was too much for me and since the only time I could truly forget was in Crow's arms, I reached for it.

Or maybe this connection was so strong it wouldn't let me pull away from him. This was all so damn confusing and since I got on the back of his bike, I was in it now and needed to figure this shit out.

The bottom line was I wanted to be with this man and cared for him deeply. Everything else would either come or it wouldn't. We'd have to cross that bridge when it got to us. I couldn't put the cart before the horse as the old saying went.

Pulling up to the emergency room, lights flashed and cars were parked everywhere. Wrong Way barely had the bike stopped before I was hopping off, ripping my helmet off. I had one thought, one mission.

Crow.

Running into the building, the waiting room was packed with men wearing the Ravage MC patches all blending together. Considering I only knew a few of them, one would think I'd feel out of place, except I didn't. Being around Ravage all my life came in helpful in these situations. I searched for Crow, not seeing him through the throngs of leather.

When all eyes turned to me, I tried recognizing them all with a small smile, but continued to look for Crow. Finally spotting him at the end of a row of chairs, I marched directly to him, the crowd parting as needed. None of the brothers said a word, but they didn't take their attention from me one bit. It was normal for them to feel for their brethren, and a strange woman coming up to their president warranted it. They'd protect him until their death.

The guys Crow introduced me to at the greasy spoon nodded at me as well, but said nothing. Everything was somber.

Crow's head was down, elbows to knees. I was learning this was his pose when something hit him in the feeling zone, when he couldn't take much more and just needed space. Unfortunately, he wouldn't be getting space here. Placing my hand on his shoulder, his head shot up, anguish all over him.

One look at me and he jumped up from the chair and wrapped me in his arms so damn tight I could barely breathe, his face going into my neck. This seemed to be his thing with me. Even with how tight he held me, I wouldn't push him away for anything. I held him right back trying to absorb his pain so it didn't hurt so bad. I'd been here in this exact spot when Grandpa was hit and flipped off his motorcycle.

That unknown feeling. The guessing game of what could've happened different. The what-ifs that wouldn't just shut the hell up in your head. All of it.

He was sucking in deep breaths, and each time he did it tickled my skin. This was what he needed, and I was honored to be the one to give it. We held each other there for a long time. Neither of us wanting to let go. So long the people around us began to talk in low tones.

Crow's grip on me never changed.

"Mr. Blaine's family," I heard someone speak from the side, and Crow's head popped up turning to the sound. He grabbed my hand tight and pulled me with him to the doctor, wrapping his arm around my shoulders and pulling me in close to his side. A place I was coming to love.

He was young, like Doogie Houser young. I watched the TV reruns sometimes, sue me. It was a good show.

The devastating news was written all over his face. He tried to mask it, but did a shit job at it. It was one job I'd never want to do in my lifetime. Breaking families up and learning to grieve, no thank you. My heart ached, cracked, and bled for Crow. He was going through so much and add this to the mix of feelings he was trying to deal with, I was surprised he was able to hold himself together. It just spoke to the strength that was Crow.

"I'm his son," Crow said, pulling me into him tighter, and I wrapped my arms around his waist giving him comfort, or at least trying. At least he knew I was here for him and that was all anyone could do at this point. His brothers gathered around us.

"We did everything we could do, but we couldn't save him." Crow jerked like the doctor hit him in the gut with a sledgehammer. If he didn't bend over and puke, I'd be surprised. Even tough men had feelings, and losing a loved one was one of those that never felt good or went away. Another thing we had in common, and I hated that for him. "He suffered a heart attack, but with his condition, he didn't have long." The man carried on with his voice cracking a bit under the weight of what he was telling all of us.

"What do you mean?" Crow asked, his hand tightly gripping my shoulder.

The doctor looked at Crow like he was crazy. Like he should know something that he obviously didn't. "The new protocol meds with chemo treatment wasn't working to get rid of the cancer. He was only given a few more months to live. Add in his previous heart condition and the odds were not in his favor."

This time Crow let me go and crashed into a chair that groaned in protest with his weight. He was stunned, shaken, and shattered. A feeling I knew all too well and hadn't diminished one bit. I knew that pain and hurt. There was nothing I could do for

Crow but be there for him. That was all anyone could do.

The doctor kept talking, looking down at Crow who was unfocused. "We won't be doing an autopsy."

"Doesn't fuckin' matter. He's gone," Crow said immediately.

"I'm very sorry for your loss," the doctor said quickly and left the waiting room, everyone standing there stunned by the news.

I fell in the seat next to him, but didn't touch him. Some people needed to be alone to figure things out. While others needed comfort. If Crow needed me, he knew I'd be there for him. Everyone grieved differently, and you had to respect that.

"Sophia, now's not the time," I heard a male voice say and turned to it. The woman next to him was gorgeous, beyond beautiful. Long chestnut hair that fell down her back like a sheet of satin and glowed in the fluorescent lights of the room. Perfect eyes that were wide and lashes long. She had on a t-shirt and jeans, but you would've thought she was walking the runway. There was nothing about her that screamed biker chick at all, but she was something to Crow.

Brewer stepped in her path just as I heard Greer. "I want to see my dad."

Shit. That was Greer's mother. That meant Crow was with this beauty of a woman. Jealousy had never been my thing, but hell it was hard to turn off that nasty switch. She was beyond words. Why in the world did he have me in his bed, when he had that?

"Let 'em," Crow said from the chair, not getting up, the blow too much for him. Greer sat next to him on the other side, and only then did Crow turn to his son. It was uncanny the resemblance between them. Yet, I wasn't sure where Greer got that vicious attitude from. Crow never showed me that side of him, but being a teenager myself, I knew we could all have issues.

"He's gone, boy. Heart attack." Greer's face twisted in disbelief and hurt, but as he looked around the room at all the men in it, he locked it down somehow. That was hard for a full-grown adult let alone a young boy to do. It was something that actually impressed me and, let's be honest, the kid had a long way to go for that.

"Crow." Sophia's voice was delicate like a flower ready to bloom in the spring. A song that could cure worldwide famine or diseases.

Crow rose and wrapped Sophia in his arms exactly how he did me only moments ago burying his face in her neck as well. She returned it holding him close. The knife sliced through my heart in one go. That want or need he had, it wasn't for me and me only. It wasn't my neck he wanted to be buried in. It was for anyone who would console him with all the agony he was feeling.

Fuck. That killed, but like everything else, I pushed it down.

I refused to allow the bitterness and pain to win. Not right now anyway.

It wasn't the time to be feeling this way, but the crushing feeling was more real than I'd ever experienced. They had a story I wasn't privy to. It was long and deep with a child in the mix. It also made me feel like a third wheel, something I didn't like one bit.

Crow pulled back, and Sophia's eyes came to mine. Surprise then shock registered in them, but neither of us said anything.

I knew what I thought though. *Get your fucking hands off of him.* At least that was my first reaction. There was this instant feeling to erase Crow and Sophia's history together because she meant something to him.

It wasn't my place, and it wasn't the time.

Instead, she turned and spoke to Crow who still had his hands on her arms. "You need to go home and start making plans. If you need my help I'm a phone call away."

"Thanks, Soph," Crow responded, giving her arms a squeeze. Couldn't say that didn't score a direct hit either, but it did. She was a comfort to him and had been in his life for at least sixteen years. That was a lot of history. It scored inside my heart. She loved him. She wanted him. She needed him.

Insecurity built inside me. This was an uncommon emotion for me. Like a seed being watered, the feelings grew the more I studied Sophia and Crow.

She had a piece of him.

And I had no doubt that she would have him again.

CHAPTER FIVE

Crow

DEATH. EACH ONE OF US IN THE RAVAGE MC KNEW THE score signing on to be in this club. There was a risk the reaper would come calling, especially with the fucked-up shit we did to earn a living. That the deals we made could turn on us at any given time. That allies could become enemies in a flash.

Even knowing all of that, it didn't matter the club won out.

Except none of that took him from me. None of that took him from us. He was once a leader in this club. He was a solid man and gave me a foundation to build my life on.

Now though he was gone. It could've happened anytime from anything.

Still, that knowledge didn't lessen the blow of losing someone and having them wiped off the earth forever. No matter how you looked at it, death was official. Final and all-consuming in the grief department.

Sitting on the couch with a beer in my hand, my eyes stared at the television not seeing a damn thing that played on the screen. Rylynn's head laid on my stomach, her fingers drawing small circles under my shirt.

The touch was nice, but I couldn't find the comfort in it because the guilt was overrunning me. The knowledge that telling my dad he wasn't my biological father was too much for him. It was what caused his heart attack. It was selfish of me to want to know if he knew about it and push him like I did.

If I hadn't, he would still be here and we'd get to enjoy a few more months with him. There would be no plans being made to bury him into the ground. There would be no celebration being set up to honor him.

He'd be here sitting on the couch, watching a game, and getting to meet Rylynn. Now, he'd never meet her. He'd never see his grandkids grow up and become the adults they would one day become. Fuck, that hurt so damn bad and knowing I played a role in it, fucking killed.

The doorbell rang. Rylynn rolled off me, my sweatpants having a very difficult time staying up on her. She was tiny compared to me. "Got it," she called, and I kept quiet.

My brothers wanted to come over tonight, but I

told them I needed some quiet. They respected that, even put measures in place to keep it that way.

Rylynn opened the door with one of her beautiful smiles. The delivery guy smiled wide back at her as she handed him some cash and took the bags from him with a "Thanks." She shut the door and locked it. Even telling her a hundred times that I wasn't hungry she insisted on getting food.

There was no energy left to argue. She wanted to try to feed me, so be it. Didn't mean any of it would be touching my mouth.

Rylynn shuffled off to the kitchen where plates and silverware clanked around.

The front door opened once more, and I heard Rylynn, "Here, Ethan. Thanks for keeping a lookout."

"Thanks," he responded and she shut the door, locking it once again. Since telling the guys I needed to be alone, they put Ethan out on watch to kick people to the curb. The fact that Rylynn was taking care of him too, showed of her character and was one more thing to love about her. This was a life few understood. This was a life not many women could fit into, but she did and she did it well.

When she came to the living room with two plates full of Chinese food, I didn't want it.

Surprisingly, she didn't pressure me. Instead, she set the plate on the small table where we kept the remotes, then sat back in the couch with her plate and began to eat.

The smell hit me, and my stomach rumbled. Fuck. I was hungry. Reaching over, I snatched the plate up and began eating chicken, beans, and rice. Again, Rylynn said nothing, just let me do my thing at my own pace. She didn't have a smartass comment about how she was right or anything. Her restraint was admirable.

The food was good, but didn't stop the emptiness I felt. Again, without a word, Rylynn took my plate and hers into the kitchen, coming back with two beers. She handed one to me, and it was half gone in the blink of an eye.

In my life, there were lots of crazy things I'd had to do. Never once did anything ride on me like this, making me feel guilty and lost. I'd always been one to know what I wanted and went for it. Right now, I just didn't know what end was up and what was down.

Rylynn took her spot back on the couch, laying her head on my abs, my fingers going into her hair. They sifted through over and over again.

"I feel like my world has been rocked to the point that I don't know who I am anymore." The words came out quiet, but held so much meaning.

Rylynn's head didn't move and when she didn't say something right away, I thought she'd gone to sleep. Then she spoke. "You know exactly who you are, Crow.

You've spent thirty-three years becoming the man you are today. Your dad knew who you were and wanted you to run the club."

"How'd you know that?"

"People talk." She shrugged. "Everything you are today is because of your father, this club, and your experiences. While finding out the truth of your biology was a blow, it didn't change one thing about the father you've known for thirty-three years."

My fingers stilled for a moment then started again. "If I wouldn't have questioned him about it, he wouldn't have had the heart attack." There, I finally allowed the words to tumble out.

She shifted, her chin twisting so she met my eyes. "Don't do that to yourself." She paused as if she was truly thinking through her next words. "When my grandpa was killed, he was out on a family ride celebrating Pops and that he made it through his heart attack and being shot. All out enjoying the weather. Then a car runs into his trike sending two people flying in the air." She pauses.

"Now what if Pops needed another day to recover and the ride wasn't until the next day. Or what if my grandpa decided not to go that day and stayed home. Or what if it rained instead of it being sunny. All the what ifs will drive you batshit crazy, Crow. I know. I've thought of every single one of them, replaying the last things I said to him, what could I have said to keep him away from the ride? But you know what, I've come to a conclusion. There was nothing that could have been different, and it happened exactly as it was supposed to have. Does it rip my heart out, yes. Will it rip me apart for a long time, yes. But living with the guilt of could've, would've, should've isn't what your dad would want for you."

Needing oxygen, I sucked in a deep breath but it did nothing to soothe the ache inside. "I feel like I killed him." The weight was holding me down, the room was closing in. Hell, every breath was harder and harder to take.

Rylynn moved quickly off me, kneeling in front of me her hands to both sides of my cheeks forcing me to pay attention to her. "You did no such thing, Crow. Listen to me right now. Life has strange ways of working, but I believe down to my soul that you did not cause your father's death. A faulty heart and cancer killed your father. He loved you. I can tell by the way you talk about him. He would not want you to carry this on your shoulders or feel this even a tiny bit. Don't let his death be in vain."

I pressed my lips to hers needing her connection, and she opened up freely. She allowed me to give and take in that kiss. When I pulled away, her eyes were dilated and fully aroused. She blinked quickly swiping it away. Another thing to love about this woman.

"Get up here and let's finish watching whatever in the hell's on TV."

She smiled up at me then jumped up and resumed her position. That was exactly how we fell asleep.

"W<small>HAT CAN</small> I <small>DO FOR YA</small>?" Brewer asked, sitting down on my couch on one end with Wrong Way moving to the other. Beers in hand, I sucked in the day. It was strange waking up to a new dawn, a new start, then feeling the rush of grief come through like a hurricane and nail you down once again.

"Bear and Goldi are handlin' most of it. When they have questions, they'll call. We're shootin' for it to happen in the next couple of days and give time to the other charters to make it down if they want to come. Van's with Goldi, and Greer's at his mom's. Other than that, I'm keepin' on keepin' on."

"That man loved you, Crow. You gotta know that." Brewer had known my dad for as long as I had. He was always around our house saying he was my brother. What he didn't know though, was what I did. What caused my dad to get his heart thumping so hard it stopped altogether.

It was time. These two men knew everything about me, and this would be no different.

"This is between the three of us."

Breaking the last few days down for my brothers, they didn't say a word once I'd finished. Therefore, I didn't know their reaction to it. It meant something to me how they felt. They were my brothers, best friends, and had been with me through the worst of shit. What they felt mattered.

"Know you're thinkin' it's your fault," Brewer started, leaning forward, elbows to knees, face on me. It was his 'listen to me' position that he'd honed in on for years. "It's not. That's some heavy shit, and you needed to know if your old man knew. Can't put that on you, brother."

I chuckled.

"What's funny?" Wrong Way asked, his brow tipped as if I'd lost my mind.

"Rylynn said the same thing last night."

"She's a smart woman. Where is she?" Wrong Way questioned, picking his boot up and crossing it over his knee. He was more laid back than Brewer, but he always had my back.

"Sent Ethan to drive her around and get some clothes and whatever else she needed. She'll be back soon."

Brewer coughed once. "The way that woman jumped on your bike, Crow, was somethin' else. She saw your face and didn't think twice about what she was doin'. Didn't care she had nothin'. The only thing she gave a shit about was you."

"You back to giving advice? Maybe we should call you Cupid."

He sat up. "Whatever works."

I felt my lip tip, and it felt strange. After feeling so down the last day to actually smirk again felt foreign. I didn't know if that was a good thing or something else to feel guilty for.

"Any club news I need to know?"

"Well…" Brewer started, and I lifted my hand.

"Talk to me. Just because I was down a day doesn't mean I'm not the fuckin' president of this club. You do not handle me with kid gloves." My tone was sharper than normal.

"Brother," Wrong Way said, sitting up, apparently ready for me to take a swing at Brewer, not that I would. At least not right now.

"Got it. Besides the two cameras at the store, we've found nothing else. Tommy's ass hasn't gotten in touch about the info on the people tailin' us or Barry," Brewer said.

"We even sure there is a someone tailin' us?" I asked, knowing my guys knew when eyes were on them. They'd been doin' this shit for too long not to, but if there were cameras, it meant eyes.

Brewer shrugged. "Who the fuck knows, but we're keepin' everything current and flyin' under the radar."

I nodded.

"Hornet found a guy to replace Carlo. Has him comin' at the end of the week to get okayed by you. He's been vetted, and we've all taken a very close look at him. Damien is a very low-level player, and Xavier was right. He's trying to take over his territory. Tex says Stephanie is good, back to her tricks, but no Barry," Brewer continued.

He paused as Wrong Way took over. "Kenny's got nothin' on the money from Barry's house."

"Not surprising. The woman wouldn't be bitchin' about bills if she knew there was that much money in the house," I added on, leaning back into the couch.

Wrong Way continued, "The Purple Pride is somethin' we need to take a closer look at. Their shit is non-existent for the most part. The building is under a holding company's name, and it's buried deep. Still lookin' for it. Tex and Phoenix rode up there, went in and had a drink at the bar. Didn't see anything out of the ordinary except a large barn outside of it. Really, came back with nothin'. Didn't see Sophia's man up there either."

My fingers running through my hair, I replied, "This bunch of nothin' shit's ending. What about Ebony?" I asked, needed to make sure Jenny's shit was over with. She needed to clean up and stay her ass in rehab. It also meant I was stuck cleaning her shit up.

Wrong Way spoke, "Phoenix tried callin' her. She didn't pick up, but one of her assholes did. Said she was out of town and would be back next week. Asked him about the house, didn't know a damn thing."

No shit he wouldn't know. Ebony kept a tight hold on her business.

"Keep your pulse on all of it and keep me updated. Any buyers for the guns?" They needed to get gone from the basement under the convenient store. It was one more thing we didn't need hangin' over our heads, and if someone was watching, needed to be gone.

Wrong Way shifted in his chair and looked over to Brewer, the movement making me become more alert. "Wells said he'll take the hands for full price value." Brody Wells had a crew in the southern tip of Alabama, by Mobile. Wells' crew was able to get product off the Gulf and had proven over the years to be a trustworthy ally.

I nodded because that was a given. "That's good."

"Starling said he'll take the ARs and AKs."

My body went still. Erik Starling was on the opposite end of the spectrum when it came to our relationship. It was rocky at best and fucking mountains at there. No way in fuck this was happening. "You mean to tell me you fuckin' called him about this shit?"

Wrong Way's back straightened. "Word on the street was he was lookin'. He called us. The thing is, he'll pay us triple what they're worth."

Anger flooded me. It was a damn good deal, but no way in fuck would we sell our shit to that snake. "No.

Find someone else. I don't give a fuck if we have to take a hit on selling the fuckin' things. We're not sellin' to Starling." He was a piece of shit who turned on us years ago. Ravage didn't forget that shit. Ever. The fact they brought this to me was actually surprising. I'd expected them to already know this answer. If we were hurting for the money, it may be a consideration. But just to get stock out, I'd figure something out.

"Got it," Wrong Way said, looking over at Brewer.

"What the fuck is with the looks? Just spit this shit out so we can get it done with."

Brewer took one for the team and spoke, "Just think about Starling." I went to talk, but he kept on going. "It's half a million dollars, Crow. Know he's a dick, but we gotta think about what's best for the club."

"What, you think arming those dickheads with weapons is smart? What if Starling gets another bur up his ass and wants to come after us? We don't have double stock to protect us, therefore we're fucked."

"I get you, brother," Brewer said as I looked to Wrong Way.

"Are we in the hole so fuckin' much we need to do this shit?" While I knew the answer to this shit, getting down to the real reason this was even an issue was the goal.

He answered, "We're good. Understand what you're sayin' about Starling. What if the sale of them is contingent on something?"

"And what would that be?" I asked, curious.

Brewer answered instead, "Make an agreement. We keep a tight hold on it. He crosses one line we take him out."

While I knew this shit was coming from a good place, selling to Starling didn't feel right.

"He won't keep it," I declared, sitting back in the couch. "What's really goin' on here?"

Wrong Way and Brewer looked at one another, and that was starting to piss me off.

"Just don't wanna get caught with 'em. And right now, he's the only buyer," Wrong Way put in.

"We're not in this shit for greed. We'll sit on it for right now. Not doing shit right now but protecting our own. We're goin' through the next few days, then back to the grind." The shit of my life was too much to make a final decision on it, plus, we needed to have church before we went forth with either of them. Now wasn't the time for that. But I doubted very highly my opinion would change.

"Got it."

The door swung open and Rylynn stepped through, hands covered in bags with Ethan on her heels carrying bags of his own. She looked sexy as hell in new jeans and a top that made her hair glow.

"Have fun doin' girly shit, Ethan?"

Ethan turned to us and smiled. "She likes to try on shit."

A growl came deep in my throat as I leapt from the couch and charged at Ethan. Rylynn got between him and I, her hand on my chest.

"He was just joking, Grizzly. Calm your shit. And I only tried on the bras and panties for him."

Rounds of laughter could be heard, and I felt the anger push through. A day without her smartass and I missed it. It felt right. It felt like home. Leaning down I kissed her hard. "You really want me to beat your ass."

She got on her tiptoes. "You keep sayin' it, but never do it. All bark and no bite."

"Everyone out," I ordered, swiftly gripping Rylynn by the thighs and hoisting her up my body. She squealed, and I heard the men in the room laugh.

I turned, not seeing them move. "Now!"

"Don't make it too red. Want her to be able to sit at some point in the next few days," Wrong Way joked as he left followed by Brewer and Ethan.

I marched us over to the door, locked it and slid the chain on as well.

"What's this about?" Rylynn asked as we moved swiftly through the house. My bed was front and center in the room. My cock hardened thinking of Rylynn and her noises in my bed for the first damn time. Last night falling asleep on the couch, we didn't make it this far.

Today, I was hard, and she needed to be spanked.

"All bark and no bite. Huh?" I asked, sitting on the bed so she straddled me.

Her smile gave it away. "I've had worse bites from a kitten."

On a growl, I captured her lips, my hand going to her back and pushing her into me. Her hips began to swivel, hardening my cock.

"Oh no you don't." My arms held her up pushing her to her feet.

She stood with her hands on her hips. "Umm... am I missing something here? Guess so." Ry made a turn to leave, but I caught her by the waist and reached in front to unbutton then unzip her jeans.

"Off."

"No," she said flat out. "Make me." Her ass pressed hard into my dick as she gave it a little shake, challenging me. Fuck yes.

Turning us quickly, I flung her to the bed, grabbed her ankles then jeans and pulled them down. Whipping them off, I stopped.

Rylynn had on a see-through scrap of fabric that had black lace adorning the sides. Fuck it was hot. She smiled knowing she got me and tried to squirm off the bed. Grabbing her ankle once again, I sat and put her over my knee, one leg covering both of hers to lock her down.

Her ass was on full display. Fuck, she looked good in a thong. Round and plump.

Squeezing the cheeks of her ass, she moaned. Fuck yeah. She was getting off on this shit too.

Her hand came up as her back arched, trying to get away from me. Therefore, I locked her hands behind her back and gripped them with one hand.

"You do realize you're still barking and not biting."

Lifting my hand, it hit her hard. She jolted up and cried out. "No bite huh?"

Her breaths became more labored. "Still barking," she taunted.

In rapid succession, one cheek then the other until ten was reached.

"Oh, my God," she groaned, and I grazed my fingers over her pussy. Soaked. Drenched. Fuck, that was hot. She tried wiggling her ass, then I took my fingers away.

"Is my girl turned on?"

Her head fell down, and her body went slack. "Just fuck me."

I chuckled. "Now what fun would that be?" My fingers went back to lightly graze her pussy lips, while I watched my red marks turn deeper on her ass. My cock could pound nails.

She wiggled again. "I feel you. You want my wet pussy just as much as it wants your cock."

Another growl escaped me as I flipped her to her feet. She swayed, but I kept her steady with one hand while releasing my dick with the other. Pulling him out, her eyes dilated. She wanted to suck me off.

That would be for another time.

Grabbing her arm, I pulled her to straddle me once again, and as she went down her hot heat covered me. I bucked my hips and pushed so fucking deep inside her she'd remember a few hours from now where she'd been.

She cried out, her hands gripping my shoulders as she got leverage with her knees. Then she rode. The combination of her movements and my deep thrusts up was too much. Way too much.

Her eyes were beginning to close, and I knew she was almost there. With my open palm, I ground down on her clit hard and watched as she set off like a rocket.

Her head fell back as the noises escaped her lips. A few more thrusts and I went right along with her.

Our breathing ragged, I fell to the bed taking her with me still deep in her. She lay on my chest, her hair getting caught by the slight sheen on her forehead.

She moved and rested her chin on my chest. "Next time, I spank you."

This made me laugh full out, body shaking. "Love to see you try that one."

"Oh, it's gonna happen."

The smile still covered my face. "Pixie, you pin me down to the bed, then I'll gladly take your ass beating. But, babe, chances of that shit are zero."

Her mouth twisted as she touched her finger to her chin as if thinking. "You'd be surprised what I can do."

Pulling her up, I shut her up with my lips and she fell into me making us once again breathless.

She collapsed back to my t-shirt covered chest. It was hot we were still dressed and fucked that hard. This woman turned me inside out.

As we laid there the world decided to come crashing down, and my mood changed. She felt it as she reached over and grabbed my hand lacing her fingers through it.

"Know you feel guilty for laughin' and havin' sex."

How did this woman know me so damn well? I gave her a squeeze in response.

She let out a sigh. "It's a raw wound right now, Crow. It will be for a while. But do you think for one second that your dad wouldn't want to see you smile? That's what we just did. Lift some of the bad shit at least for a little bit so when the next moment comes and we have to deal once again, we're a little bit ready for it because we had a break."

"You sure you're not like sixty-years-old?"

She lifted her head and quirked her brow. "I'm hoping this asinine comment was just a fluke."

I chuckled. Yes, again. "You're wise beyond your years, Rylynn. You seem to know the exact right thing to say when I need it."

She licked her lips. "An old soul."

"Yeah."

The way she looked at me, like I was all she'd ever need, struck me hard in the chest. So hard it made me realize the pain that my father must've felt when he had his attack. It was that potent. Didn't like comparing it, but what Rylynn was giving me right now was a shot to the heart.

"You're beautiful."

She bit back her retort and before she could say anything, the doorbell rang.

"Guess it's time to see people," I told her, brushing her hair behind her ear. "You're fuckin' perfect, Rylynn."

Her smile was wide as she leaned down and kissed me hard. "Need to clean up." On that, her hot little ass walked away to the bathroom. Damn, fucked her with her underwear still on. Fuck, I loved that shit.

Lifting from the bed, I buttoned my pants and went to the door. Opening it, Goldi stood there with a sad smile on her face.

"Daddy!" Van called out, running right into me. I took a moment to feel my daughter. Loved her with everything I had. I was also pissed at myself that I didn't force Jenny to go to rehab sooner. It was something to make up for with Van.

"Hey, peanut. How are ya?"

She looked up at me, her brown eyes glistening. "Grandpa's really dead?"

I kneeled down and went eye to eye with her. "Yeah. He had a heart attack."

"Will you have that?" she asked quickly.

"No, baby. It was just his time I guess."

A tear slid down her cheek. I pulled her into my arms and let her cry. Goldi appeared to have the same problem.

She smiled down at us. "Need to do a few things then Bear and I'll be back."

"Thanks."

"Anytime," she said, moving out of the door and shutting it.

Van lifted up. "I don't like this," she said matter-of-factly.

"I don't either."

I felt Rylynn before I saw her. Van's eyes got wide.

"Hey," Rylynn said as I picked Van up bringing her eye level with Rylynn. "What's your name?"

My little girl not missing a beat answered, "Van."

"Well hi, Van. I'm Rylynn." Rylynn held out her hand, and Van took it shaking it softly.

"You're really pretty," Van told her, making Rylynn laugh.

"And you're gorgeous," Rylynn responded with a bop on Van's nose.

"Is this your girlfriend, Daddy?" Van asked. Loved the innocence. Even with all the shit she'd seen, she was still my little girl.

I felt Rylynn get tight beside me and I didn't know why, but I responded. "Yep."

"Are you getting married?"

This made Rylynn burst out laughing once again. She didn't answer, but I did. "Not tomorrow, munchkin'."

"Oh," Van said.

"Why don't you take your bag into your room and get unpacked."

Van bent and kissed my cheek. "Okay."

I set her down to her feet, and she looked at Rylynn. "Nice to meet you." She then took off down the hall.

"Wow," Rylynn said.

"What do ya think?" I asked, wrapping my arms around her and pulling her close to me.

"I think being with you is going to be an adventure."

Kissing her hard, I pulled back. "Welcome to the ride."

Yeah, Rylynn wasn't going anywhere.

CHAPTER SIX
Rylynn

Opening the door once again, more smiling faces that I kept welcoming into Crow's home arrived. We'd run out of room in his freezer and fridge with all the damn casseroles people brought over.

Death equaled food in my experience. Since we were overloaded with them, I had the oven on and when one came, I put it in there, heated it up, and put it out for all to eat. Hell, any other food that came I did the same.

It worked well.

Keeping busy was good.

Van helped me as much as she could, setting out plates and silverware. She was cute as a button, and instantly I loved her. She had none of the attitude Greer had in her, thank Christ.

A couple kids showed up so then she went back

and forth between helping me and playing. Even when I told her to play, she still made it a point to come and help. I enjoyed her assistance and watching her move about the space comfortably. I imagined this was how my mother felt watching me and the others as children.

Family was more than the blood in your veins and your DNA. Ravage was family, and I found comfort that Crow had this.

Starting to move away from the door, the bell rang once more. It didn't piss me off that this had become my role one bit. Having a smile on my face while I answered the door was no loss to me. If this was how I could help, then I was truly happy to do so. It was the number of people all cramming into the house that gave me hesitation, and I was used to a lot of people. But at this rate, this house was going to burst at some point, but it was what Crow wanted, and I'd do anything just about now to get him to be happy.

Warmth hit my back, and I looked up to see Crow right behind me. He leaned down to my ear. "Thanks for doin' this, Pixie." Then kissed the shell of my ear sending chills down my spine. That right there made it all worth it.

Swinging the door open, a beautiful woman with almond eyes, long curly hair, and tits so big they were bursting out of the small top she wore stood there. "Hi..." I started as she squealed and rushed past me in a whoosh and into Crow's arms, wrapping hers around his neck and pressing her body against his.

"And Malibu Barbie enters the fun," I muttered under my breath as the door shut.

"I just can't believe it," the woman whined, looking up at Crow like she wanted to eat him for breakfast. Maybe she wanted it to sound like she was crying or sad, but it didn't come out that way one bit. It was worse than nails on a chalkboard. I already didn't like her.

Crow tried to unwrap the woman's hands from around his neck, but she wouldn't let go. "He's gone, Crow. What am I going to do?" Cue more of the dramatics. The woman would never win an acting award, that was for sure. Made me wonder if this chick even liked Crow's father. It wouldn't surprise me one bit if she didn't. That wasn't a catty thing, it was a real thing. Seeing this shit happen, women doing anything to get a man, that was exactly what this was. A play.

"Kara, know you're hurting. Dad liked you a lot and appreciated you taking him where he needed to go."

She pulled back, but kept very close. Too close. Her damn tits were going to pop if she got any closer to him. If I had a knife in my hand, I'd pop the fuckers. Note to self: start carrying.

Crow was trying to be nice, but the tightness of his jaw told me he didn't like this one bit.

"He meant the world to me. I just don't know what I'm going to do without him."

Yeah, her acting skills beyond sucked. Her transparency was crystal clear, and it pissed me off.

If I punched her the day after the man I was sleeping with dad's died, would I go to hell for that? Who was I kidding, there was already a flame with my name on it. But causing a scene wasn't top on my agenda list for the day. What the hell...

"Kara, let go," Crow ordered, but the woman wouldn't give up carrying on and continuing to get up in his space. Crow was strong and could easily remove this chick's arms, but was trying to be nice. No one here needed to see him detonate. He'd been holding his shit together well, but there was always that risk of it going bad fast. It would only take one thing to set off the fireworks. Not on my watch.

Huffing out a breath, I moved to Crow's side. "You didn't tell me your dad babysat."

Kara's lip curled and since I was done listening to her whine, I moved fast, grasping her wrists, twisting them, and putting her down on her knees. "When a man tells you to let go, you fuckin' let go."

Her eyes were a blaze of fury, but I was past caring what she thought. If I did, then my hands would've stayed to myself.

"You bitch!" she spat as I released her hands and took a step back.

Looking over to Crow, his eyes were wide. "What? You think I don't pack a mean punch? Told ya I could take care of myself." I gave him a small wink as Kara tried to stand up. Too bad her shoes were so damn high it made the task very difficult and the crotch shots from her short skirt were less than desirable. Cameltoe through the thong, yuck.

Crow grasped my hand and pulled me to his side, kissing me hard in front of everyone in the room. When he pulled away I asked, "Please don't make this an everyday thing with your hotness. Teaching every woman in Rebellion a lesson wasn't what I came here for."

His hand cupped my cheek, and I freaking loved that move. It was so intimate. Even with all the people around us, they didn't exist. It was only us. Nothing else mattered.

"You're the shit," he said softly.

I tapped my finger to my cheek. "You've told me that a time or two."

He kissed me hard then looked at Kara. "You can go."

She huffed, "I have a right to be here! More than her."

This made me chuckle because she was probably right.

"I don't need any more shit, Kara. Just go."

She finally made it to her feet. "Fine. I'll go just for

you so I don't lay that bitch out."

My body tensed, and Crow gripped my shoulder hard anticipating my movement. It was the only thing that stopped me. She turned and walked out the door. Fucking hell.

I turned in Crow's arms. "Sorry about that."

"No, you're not." He smiled down at me, and it was a gift. I'd missed the smiles and the easygoing nature about him. It was a good look that I'd craved since our last meeting.

With a shrug, I said, "Not really."

The party continued and people kept coming in, but not as many were leaving making the room get smaller and smaller.

It was three hours later when the next situation happened. I was sitting on the couch with a woman named Goldi when the doorbell went off again. After awhile, Crow set Jimmy on to be the opener saying I needed a break. Truthfully, I was happy for the reprieve and to get off my feet for a bit.

Goldi, short for Goldilocks, was in her late fifties or early sixties, beautiful with her golden hair. She'd been in the club for years and was the ol' lady to a bur of a man named Bear. He looked as if he could crush you by just thinking about it.

"Girl, then you know how it is with these men." She shook her head smiling. "Gotta be bad asses all the time."

I smiled, really liking this woman. "The way of the world." Goldi asked me if I was familiar with the MC life, and I couldn't help but chuckle. When I got done with my story, she reached for my hand and squeezed it once. I'd like to think it was in approval.

"But, girl. You need to call your daddy. I bet he's tearin' shit up. I've met Rhys, and he's not a man to be fucked with."

"I will. Just giving it time." The plan was to call home tonight and tell everyone what had happened. Dad would be pissed, but Cruz for sure would want to know.

She took a pull on her beer. "Don't give it too much time. Crow'll have no qualms about goin' toe to toe with that man. Just make it as easy as possible. That's what we do for our men. Lessen the blow so it doesn't get to the point of no return."

What she said to me really stuck, and part of me felt like there was a lead weight in my gut. "I'm not sure I'll be stayin' around here, Goldi."

"That man can't keep his eyes off you."

Looking over to Crow, who was talking to his brothers, he lifted his chin at me, and I smiled. Life couldn't be that simple. I didn't trust it. Couldn't. Smooth had never been the Ravage way.

"I..."

"Crow!" A woman's voice came from the doorway catching my attention. What? Did the Ravage men have a criteria check? If you're hot come on by. Tits and ass, sign me up! This woman was all legs and tits, wild brunette hair and enough makeup to keep Bozo happy for a year. But it wasn't just her.

Behind her came seven other women. All beautiful and knowing they were. Crow smiled warmly to them and gave each a hug. One had dark shadows under her eyes that could still be seen under her makeup.

That damn green-eyed monster wanted to come out and stake her claim, but I kept myself in my seat. I'd already called attention to myself once, no need for an encore.

They pawed over him making sure to give extra-long hugs. Crow didn't seem to mind one bit, another thing I was letting go.

Fuck, when did I become so possessive of this man?

Probably the moment you got on the back of his bike and came to Rebellion, idiot.

"Oh, the girls are here." Goldilocks jumped up from her seat and began to hug each of the women like she'd known them all their lives. She might have, how would I have known. She took extra time with the one with the dark circles who smiled back at Goldi.

They stood around in their mini huddle for quite some time. It was the only time during the day when I felt out of place. Like there was something I should know, but didn't. Instead of marching over and making my presence known, along with everything else I let it roll off my back.

It wasn't easy, but Crow didn't bring them over to me to introduce, and I kept busy with Van. She was my little savior and didn't even know it.

When they left, I felt relief which was strange. I didn't get jealous. I didn't get possessive. I didn't shove bitches off of men. At least I never did because there was never anyone to have these feelings for. Fuck.

The next thing happened an hour later as I was standing in the crook of Crow's arm, my hands on his abs as he talked to his brothers, jumping in every so often with my two cents. His body stilled, and I felt it immediately. Peering up at him, his focus was on the door. Therefore, mine went there as well.

Yet another woman came in. Surprise, surprise. This one looked as though she'd seen the end of a needle one too many times. Her skin showed years of drug abuse, hair wiry even though she tried to brush it. As she talked, several of her teeth appeared to be missing. Definite drug addict.

She stumbled around a bit, and Crow was pissed.

"Mommy!" Van cried out, running to the woman and wrapping her little arms around her legs. The woman just patted her back a couple of times. My heart clenched for Van. This was her mother? That sweet little girl was living with this woman? That just couldn't possibly be.

The wiry woman came up to Crow. Since I happened to be standing next to him, me too.

"I'm sorry," she said, and it came out very sketchy like in a way that it hurt her to say it, and she wanted something for that small bit of sympathy.

"What the fuck are you doing here?" Crow bit off harshly.

The woman's eyes skated around the room, coming back to Crow. "I just wanted to tell you sorry."

"Your ass is supposed to be in rehab, two counties over."

"I couldn't stay there," she whined, and Van let go of her mom looking up at her. Unconditional love. That was what Van had for this woman. Down the bottom of my soul I hoped that this woman knew how Van thought of her. Then looking again, it didn't appear so. My heart constricted for the little girl.

My mother was a great mom. Kind, patient, and loving. I wanted that for Van, not whatever this was standing in front of us.

"You high?" he asked her flat out. Van got stiff. It wasn't my place and I should've kept my mouth shut, but I've had to do this many times with Mazie, getting her out of sticky conversations that she didn't need to be a part of. So I did what I do. Went with my gut. Van needed to be away from this.

"Hey, Van. Let's go check out the stuff in the oven."

Van looked perplexed, wanting to stay with her

mom and dad, but also wanting to come with me. I held out my hand, and after a few beats she came to me. I led her away, but not before I heard Crow.

"You're not livin' in the house, and don't even think of takin' Van with you."

Oh boy. That didn't sound good. Even in the kitchen I could still hear them, everyone could. It was a mess because that meant Van could too. My instincts screamed to protect the young girl, to shield her from all of this. I wanted nothing more than to hold her in my arms and never let her see her mother and father like this again. It wasn't fair.

Then again, life wasn't fair was it?

Brewer and Wrong Way caught my attention as they approached Van's mother and physically escorted her out the door. Me, I stood in front of Van knowing she could probably hear, but doing my damnedest to shield her from seeing it. No kid needed that vision of their mother like that.

"Daddy," Van called out again, and ran to my left where Crow was crouched down, her face a mask of panic. "Where's Mommy going?"

"Mommy's sick, and that's why you're stayin' here for a while."

Her head darted to the door, then back to her father. "But Mommy needs me."

This was strange coming from a child, and I didn't like what it was inferring so I kept listening.

"Remember what I told you about the medicine she takes?" Van nodded. "That kind of medicine is bad and right now, Mommy is doing bad things. I need you to be safe. So you're staying with me."

"She needs me though." Tears brimmed her eyes, and she was so close to letting them fall over. My heart hurt for her.

Crow squeezed her tightly and reassuringly. "And you need to spend time with me. I've missed you like crazy."

The little girl nodded, but you could tell her heart wasn't quite in it. Crow lifted his chin to my left where Wrong Way stood holding out his hand to Van. She took it, looked back at her dad, and was swept away into the throng of people.

Crow stood, the father mask falling completely away, and anger rippled through the room as I moved to him. "That fuckin' bitch is higher than a fuckin' kite and supposed to have her ass in rehab. Now I gotta deal with her crazy ass. Van's stayin' here. She's never goin' back if Jenny doesn't clean her ass out."

He wrapped me in his arms and held me tight. I didn't know what to think.

Insecurity was a bitch and not something I was accustomed to. Yet, the feelings were there. The doubt. The questions.

Was I staying too? And if I was, how did I fit into all of this?

CHAPTER SEVEN

RYLYNN SHUT THE DOOR AND LOCKED IT UP TIGHT. THE day was exhausting, and this wasn't even the service. People from high and low came by to give their condolences. Some I hadn't seen in years. It drained the life out of me.

It was great having people show up to lend their support, talk about my dad, and couldn't forget the shit ton of food. But toward the end, I was ready for everyone to go. I needed sleep. Tomorrow was going to be worse, and I needed all the energy I could muster.

That was when I put two fingers between my lips and whistled loudly. "Time to go, people," I called out to everyone. It didn't take long for the place to clear out.

Van was so tired. Rylynn had to walk her to bed, her arms under Van's pits.

"How ya doin'?" she asked, coming up to me and wrapping her arms around my waist. The smell of Rylynn instantly engulfed me and I couldn't stop, tucking my face inside her neck to get the full effect. Fucking loved the smell of her.

I rested my forehead on hers, holding her tight. Upon instinct, I tucked my face inside her neck, inhaling her. It was as if I could pull her inside my body and make everything disappear. It calmed me which was strange because when I was there, with my eyes closed, I felt safe in allowing myself to relax. That level of trust I had with her, that she'd have my back if my eyes were closed, moved me profoundly.

Rylynn was the only one to do this for me.

"Thanks for everything today, Pixie."

"No problem. Glad I could help." Her hands caressed the back of my neck and whether she knew it or not, she was giving me strength. Never in my life had I needed that from another human being before, but she gave it freely, wanting nothing in return. Women like that were rare.

"You know I've done some fucked up shit in my life, right?"

She nodded, taking my head with hers. This was what settled me. Rylynn didn't dig into my past. She didn't question me. She gave me simple acceptance.

Something I never had before.

"Never once needed someone. Today, I needed you."

Her body melted into mine.

"You know about my two kids now. You haven't said much about that."

She sighed. "While I would've liked for you to tell me about them instead of it being a shock, it's done. You have two kids."

"And Greer is sixteen, close to you in age. Does that bother you?"

"No, does it bother you?" she asked me back.

"Not one fuckin' bit." There was a long pause, and I waited for her.

"There are lots of things you don't know about me, Crow," she started and surprising her, I picked her up and carried her to the couch where I sat and positioned her to straddle me.

"Yeah. So tell me."

Her smile radiated the space, pushing the clouds of darkness to the side and letting that light shine through. "What exactly do you want to know?"

"Everything."

Her body gave her away, telling me she liked that answer. I laid my head back on the couch and looked into her beautiful green eyes.

When she didn't say anything, I asked, "Tell me something I'd never guess with you."

Her face turned into a mask for a moment, then it receded. "I killed someone."

While most of the time some declaration of this could shock certain people, me not so much. It was interesting to hear though. "And..." I prompted.

"This bitch was going to hurt Emery, that's GT's daughter. I was outside her place and saw what was going down, pulled out my gun and fired. Bitch went down."

Raising my hand, I tucked a lock of her hair behind her ear. "Protecting your own."

"Yeah. And I don't regret a second of it. If I had a do-over, I'd do the same exact thing, no questions asked."

Fuck, this woman had a loyalty streak in her that rivaled me and my brothers to the club. Even young, she knew who she was and her character was strong and mighty. She proved today that she'd protect what was hers by getting Kara off of me with ease. Fuck, if that didn't make my dick hard.

"I know," I replied to her. "You have the protective instinct down to a science huh?"

She chuckled. "I don't know about that, but I read the situation and do what needs to be done. When I was younger, it was the exact same thing. Assholes picking on kids at school, I'd step in."

"Really?"

"Got a couple clocks to the head for it. The first

time was seriously embarrassing. That was when my dad set up some time with me and Princess. She taught me how to duck and anticipate others moves. It took me a bit to get, but let's just say the bullies at school thought twice before being dicks."

A smile lifted my lips. "You do realize that's hot, right?"

"Everything I do is hot. When are you going to figure that out?"

The bark of laughter came out rough at first. Strange how when part of your world was destroyed that laughing could feel rusty. I looked to the hallway remembering Van.

"You shut her door?"

"Yeah."

"Did you get everything this morning?"

She nodded. "Yeah. Thanks for that. And thanks for not beating the shit out of Ethan."

"He needs to learn not to say that kind of shit to a man about his woman."

Something flashed before her eyes before she let it go. "Get that. But he was just jokin' with ya."

"Know that too, but..." I flipped her on her back and pressed her into the couch with my weight. "No one fucks with you, Rylynn. No one. I'll fuckin' destroy them."

"Awe. Aren't you sweet? What a woman always wants, for her man to kill for her."

My body grew tight, and I got serious. "No fuckin' shit, Pixie. No one fucks with you."

She lifted up, her mouth connecting with mine.

It took me a moment, but knew that Van slept like a log. Fucking Rylynn on the couch; she wouldn't hear a thing, and I needed her.

There was no preamble. I needed inside of her, to drown the day and get a small reprieve from all the pain that killed me inside.

We tore at each other's clothes, throwing them all down in a heap. Two seconds later, my lips were on hers as my cock slid inside of her. Her back arched, but I wouldn't let her release my eyes. She needed to feel this. Feel this connection we had.

As I thrust inside her slow then quick, repeating it over and over again, her eyes started to fill and that was when I knew she got me. She got what I was trying to tell her. As we came together, I buried my face in her neck until our breaths evened out.

After a bit, I pulled out and laid my head on her stomach. Her hands sifted in and out of my hair, comforting and soothing.

"Who were all those girls that came? Goldi was excited to see them," she asked, and I had a choice to make. It was a huge one. This life wasn't for everyone. No way in hell I'd tell Sophia we had a stable of girls. She wasn't meant for this life and would never understand such a thing. And being straight, I never even wanted to tell Sophia because she didn't get to have the inner workings of what was inside me.

With Rylynn, she was and could handle what I told her. The thing was a decision needed to be made to let her into my life, for real this time. No playing *fuck in hotels* or any of that shit. This was as real as it got between two people in my club. Telling one another the things that only stayed between them. Never saying too much but still knowing more than anyone else because she shared my bed.

Never had I given anyone that kind of knowledge to the heart of me. It had been locked up tight for so many years I felt like I couldn't breathe.

It was judgment time. Either all in or not.

"You here with me now?" I asked instead of answering her, needing to find her pulse on being here with me.

"Right here, Crow."

My arms around her got ultra-tight, and her head popped up our eyes meeting. "Not what I mean, Pixie. You in this with me. Meaning you move your shit here and we really do this."

"You asking me to move in with you, Crow?"

The words hit me hard, and I didn't understand why because that was in fact what I was doing. Asking her to come here and take a chance on me, on us. See where this could lead. And I had a damn good idea where that would be.

"Yeah. Want you here with me."

"Can we talk about this later?" she asked, surprising me. There'd been a shit ton of women who would do anything to be in my bed. Hell, in my house. No women came here I was sleeping with ever. This place was different for me. Home. A place where I wanted to share my life.

Her wanting to talk about it later meant she wasn't ready for this step, yet every signal she'd given me said she was heading in that direction. Something wasn't right.

"What's in that head of yours?"

She got up, making me have to move, and went to the side of the couch, wrapping her arms around her knees. "I know how you feel right now. You lost someone you held close and now you want to grasp at something that's real. I get it. Really, I do. I didn't have anyone to grasp onto except you for one night the day we buried my grandpa. I just want you to be sure about this and talk about it when the pain isn't so raw."

Fuck, she was wise beyond her years. Greer would never say anything like that. He wouldn't get it one bit. She though, she did. An old soul. Fuck, she was perfect.

Sitting up, I moved over to her, picked her up, and put her in my lap. I held her tight and wrapped her in one of the blankets Van bought a while back. Her head fit right under my chin in the perfect spot. "You're right.

I am raw right now. That wound won't close for a long while, but it's also opened my eyes to what's in front of me, Rylynn. You're mine, Rylynn. Want you here with me, not in Sumner."

She said nothing, and her body began to shake. "Pixie?"

A loud pound came on the door, her eyes flying to it.

"Fuck," I ground out as she hopped up and fought with her clothes to get them on. Grabbing my jeans, I pulled them up over my ass and left them unbuttoned. Rylynn darted from the room. She wasn't the type to run, yet naked was a whole different thing when visitors were calling.

When I opened the door, I was laughing. Greer stood there, hand in a fist ready to pound once more. He halted, and Sophia was standing right behind him.

"Hey."

"Hey, Dad." Greer gave me a quick hug and moved into the house.

Sophia stepped forward, tears in her eyes. Her hands came to my cheeks, and she kissed me.

She took me by surprise, and the moment I should've stopped it—I didn't.

I also didn't know that Rylynn saw the whole thing.

CHAPTER EIGHT
Rylynn

After righting my clothes and getting presentable, I went out to greet whoever decided to show up. While I'd thought we were done for the night, we obviously weren't.

Coming to the mouth of the hall, my feet stopped as I was frozen in time. My heart squeezed to the point of physical pain.

Sophia and Crow were kissing. Her hands on his face caressing him gently.

He didn't push her away. He didn't tell her to stop.

Did I just really see that? Maybe that was it, my mind playing tricks on me.

Moving to the bedroom, I closed the door softly and went into the bathroom with my pajamas. Normally with Crow we slept naked, but part of me, the one deep inside I didn't let others see, needed a shield of some kind. It was the best I could do.

Coming out of the bathroom, the bed stared at me, taunting and teasing me. That was when I heard it, laughter coming from the living room. Daggers pierced my chest.

While I was grateful for Crow to have that humor on a day he needed it, I also hated that it wasn't me giving it to him and Sophia instead.

Turning all the lights out, I climbed into bed and pulled the sheet and blankets over me. My knees tucked up into my chest was when it happened.

The tears came, there was no stopping them. Never knew a kiss could hurt so bad, but it did.

Everything hurt.

The worst was my heart.

That was the moment I knew one hundred percent I loved him.

That I wanted to stay with him. For him to be mine.

It was also the moment I learned, some things you loved were never yours to begin with.

Somehow, I found sleep.

The dreams though, I could do without.

CHAPTER NINE
Crow

WHAT A FUCKING DAY...

Staring at the casket while Train, a brother from another charter, did the service for my father. Everything inside of me hurt, and as if Rylynn could feel it, she squeezed my hand giving me her strength. I was a selfish prick and needed her at my side even though she'd just gone through this.

Van sat beside me holding my hand as well. Greer next to her, then Sophia.

Train went on and on, but I didn't register a word that he said. All of it sounded like it was mumbles coming from somewhere else other than right in front of me. While I thought in the hospital it was real. This, seeing Dad in the coffin that would be lowered down into the ground, that was real.

He was gone. Truly gone. It didn't matter the

reason, it just was. My father always taught me that a man, a real man, should never be ashamed to show his true feelings. In my line of business, I compartmentalized it, not allowing any of the deeds that needed to be done to affect me.

This though. Seeing that fucking casket burned right into my soul. This would be a moment that I would never forget for the rest of my life. The last thing he told me was that he loved me. Christ, I knew he fucking knew I did too. It just sucked I couldn't give that to him one last time and not have it be through a damn casket.

I never once let go of my girl's hands, even when they began to sweat. I needed each of them. Rylynn grounded me, and my daughter because she meant the world to me.

Train said his final words, and we were escorted to the casket. Rylynn touched the top of it and went past, turning to look at me. Van kept a tight grasp on me, fear in her eyes. With my free hand, I lightly brushed over the casket. "Love you," I whispered, because it wouldn't come out any louder, but he needed to know one last time. He was a great father. The best. I'd miss him every day of my life.

Van did the same thing, then not looking back we went right to Rylynn. I grabbed ahold of her with one arm and dipped my head into her neck, breathing her in for a moment. She squeezed me hard and then pulled away.

She'd been a bit distant since yesterday's visit from Sophia and Greer. She never came out while they were there and when I found her later, she was in my bed asleep. With everything that had gone on, I didn't wake her. Instead, I selfishly watched her. Every inhale and exhale as if she found this special place. An untouchable moment.

It was beautiful.

She was beautiful.

This morning was chaos, and we hadn't had a chance to talk. Even though I had a thousand things I wanted to say, there just wasn't time.

"Dad. Can Mom ride with you?"

Why my son was asking this I had no idea, but it wasn't happening. That was not Sophia's place in my life. Hadn't been for a long damn time. "No. Rylynn is on the back of my bike."

"But..." Greer tried, but I cut him off.

"No, Greer. You drive her." He understood my tone and shut up quickly. A few moments later his mother came up to me, Van letting go of my hand. Then Rylynn did as well, bent down, and started talking to Van. My girl was enthralled by my woman. It hit me deep to see the way Rylynn looked at my daughter. Sophia wrapped her arms around me while my attention was on Rylynn and Van.

"I'm so sorry," Sophia said in my ear. "He was a great man who loved you more than anything. He lived a good life. Be happy about that and celebrate him, instead of mourning him."

She then pulled away from my ear.

"Thanks."

Sophia came in close and kissed my cheek. Rylynn was in an intense conversation with Van if her facial expressions were anything to go by. I smiled at Sophia and she took off with Greer, who shot daggers at me. Fucking hell. I'd deal with him later.

I was used to being pulled in a thousand different directions. It was common for more than one person to need my attention. Except the only person I wanted to focus on right now happened to be enchanted by my daughter.

Everyone came pouring out from the gravesite. Rylynn came to my ear. "My mom and dad are here along with some of my Ravage. I'll let you get to your guests."

The way she said *my Ravage* stung a little. We were all Ravage, and I wanted her to feel that my club was hers too. I decided not to dwell on it. After all, Rylynn and I were new to all of this.

She'd pulled away at the party saying she was going to call the Sumner Ravage, not that Bear hadn't already done it. It was still a nice gesture, and I didn't know how I felt about them being here.

"I'll be over there soon." I kissed the top of her head and released her as she shuttled to her family. Their eyes were on me and I lifted my chin, but it was with one that I really connected with—Cruz who was there along with Cooper, Nox, and Austyn. Shit, they all came. While this was normal for other charters to come to a member's funeral, I had a feeling this had to do more with me and my genetics.

Another thing to deal with... later.

Loads of people came up giving me their condolences. Lots of hugs, slaps on the back, and smiles. My old man was very well liked, and everyone gave him the respect he deserved.

Jenny appeared out of nowhere and grabbed Van, and I stepped in her path. "What are you doin'?"

Jenny's eyes were unfocused and crazed. "We gotta leave." She was as high as a fucking kite, or didn't have any money for her next hit. Bitch had the nerve to show up here.

"Van's not going with you."

Jenny's body stiffened. "You're not taking my girl."

"Yeah, I fuckin' am. You have no home, you're a fuckin' junkie, and Van takes more care of you than you do her. So, yeah. Until you get your shit together, that's how it'll be."

"I'd rather..." She began, but I cut her off.

"I don't give a fuck what you'd rather. Van isn't goin' anywhere with you. Either you leave quiet or you leave loud. I don't give a fuck, but either way, you're leavin' alone."

Jenny started to turn hostile, nose flaring, wrinkles on her forehead pronounced. This would be the pissed version of her that came out quite often.

She took a step forward, and I let out a whistle.

Within moments, the men from my club were right there. "Get her out of here," I ordered to anyone in the group, not giving a fuck who would do the deed. "Make sure that bitch doesn't come back or come to the clubhouse."

"Daddy. What's wrong?"

I kneeled in front of Van getting at eye level. "You're Mommy was at the doctor, but left."

"Why?"

My voice lowered. "I don't know why she left." A tear fell down her face. My daughter's pain cut me like a knife. Her mother had her warped into thinking she had to save her, care for her. That wasn't how that shit was supposed to be.

"It'll be okay."

Her cute face broke with indecision, and this was my fault. She didn't need to know at her age what a junkie looked like. She didn't need to be taking care of her mom because of addiction. Van needed a childhood, not to be pushed into adulthood way too damn early. That was the path she was going on.

That shit was done.

Van nodded as Wrong Way held out his hand to her. The man was great with kids, always wondered why he didn't have any.

"Hey, peanut. You get to ride with me." Van gave him a soft smile that barely tipped her lips, but she went with him. She loved her mom as a child should, and it killed me that she didn't have a good one. One who was more adult than child herself.

Looking off to the left, Sumner Ravage was still standing there, eyes to the crowd. Rylynn was in her father's arms, her head on his chest while he held her. Guess that shit needed to get done today too.

A chat with Rhys.

Never in a million years thought I'd be having it, but I was wrong. She was mine. She'd be mine. I wanted her here with me day and night. We had to see where this would go. If we both gave it what it needed, I knew where it would lead. Her wearing my ring and round with my baby.

Walking over to them, Cruz—or my father, fuck that was weird—was the first one to step forward and put out his hand. I shook it as he pulled me into his arms and slapped me on the back a few times. I didn't know how to feel in this moment. I'd just buried one father, now here was another giving me support. There wasn't time to process any of this.

"Sorry, Crow. Your old man was one of the best men I knew. He held your club strong for a long time.

Knew he loved you with everything he had." This declaration was strange. While I knew this information, Cruz acknowledging that my dad was really a dad in every sense of the word. It hit me in my soul, giving my dad that respect. Cruz knew how much I loved my father, and he didn't trample on any of that.

He gave me what I needed instead of any of the other shit that was swirling around us at the moment. It was much appreciated.

"Thanks."

Cooper was next. This entire experience was surreal. I had siblings. Shit.

He held out his hand and I took it, then pulled me in for a one-handed hug. "Sorry about your dad, brother. Know we got a lot of shit to hammer out, but we'll do that later. Just wanted to be here for you."

The tornado of emotions swirled around me, not exactly knowing how to feel about any of this. I just responded, "Right."

Nox was next. He did the same handshake and only the "sorry about your dad," before stepping away. Then they introduced their women. I'd met Bristyl before, but not Carsyn. She appeared like a scared rabbit, the polar opposite of Rylynn.

When it was Austyn's turn, tears rolled down her face as she launched herself into my arms. Grabbing her was my only option, and she wrapped me up tight. Her body began to shake. Christ, my sister. I had a fuckin' sister, and she was with Ryker nonetheless. I'd known Ryker for years and all the skirt he tailed. This protectiveness came over me hard and fast, and my eyes connected with his. Ryker just raised his brow, and I went back to the crying woman in my arms.

"Hey. It's okay."

She pulled away and looked up at me with red-rimmed eyes. "No. It's not okay. We should've known you were our blood. We should've been able to see you and get to know you. We should've been able to love you. But it was taken away from us." Her once tear-filled eyes were brimming with anger now. So much so I could feel her hands shake that were still touching me.

Ryker came up giving me a chin lift as he wrapped his arms around his woman. She started to fight him, but he whispered in her ear and she turned around and shook in his arms.

"She's havin' a rough time with everything," Nox said about his twin sister. "She feels like time was stolen from you, and as you can see it kills her."

"We'll have to talk about all that shit another time, man."

Nox nodded once. "Understandable."

I turned to Rhys who still had Rylynn in his arms. He was red hot with fury, but I did just like I did every other time I saw him and held out my hand. He took it and squeezed hard. I gave him the same back.

He was a big man. Not gonna lie and say he didn't scare the shit out of many a man, but I didn't back down from that shit. Never had, never would.

Rylynn's body stiffened, probably waiting for something to happen. The crash of titans. Blood spilling everywhere. The carnage of both of us lying in wait.

None of that happened. We let it go for the day. But the time would come, eventually.

"Hi, Crow." Tanner, Rylynn's mom come came up to me and Rhys' released my hand. Tanner wrapped her arms around me, hugging, then took a step back. "We're so sorry for your loss."

"Thanks."

Princess stood back and watched. This wasn't unusual for her. Whenever we'd been to their clubhouse, she did this exact thing. Taking in all the players and trying to figure out who was going to move where. We had that in common.

"Hi, Princess," I said, not letting this time pass. Time was a precious thing, and not all of us had it. No sense in making something that didn't need to be.

She stepped forward and held out her hand. I took it and she was strong, but I gave back as good as I got. She smiled. "Hi, Crow. Sorry about your dad."

"Thanks."

She let go and went into the crook of Cruz's body.

Holding out my hand to Rylynn, she came to me

immediately, and I threw my arm over her shoulder. Looking to Rhys I said, "We'll talk about this later."

His eyes turned hard seeing his daughter with me. If he wanted to do this now, we would, but I'd rather do it later.

After a few beats, he lifted his chin.

"We're all goin' to the clubhouse. Come and have a beer."

"We'll be there," Cruz said.

I led Rylynn to my bike. "Well that wasn't weird or anything," she said as she got on behind me.

"Nope. Not at all."

Now to celebrate my dad the only way he would want in a Ravage Rebellion remembrance.

CHAPTER TEN
Rylynn

THIS PARTY REMINDED ME SO MUCH OF MY GRANDPA'S. Everyone drinking and laughing, telling stories. It was a repeat and I could feel Crow's pain, because unfortunately, it was still raw inside of me.

He was a strong man, that was never in question. With each passing tick of the clock, he was getting emotionally stronger once again. The death of his father hit him hard and would for a long while, but he was getting himself back slowly. The brothers around him helped. He'd even gone off to the side and talked to Cooper and Nox, but it didn't last long because everyone was vying for his attention.

Men and women kept him busy, along with the bottles that seemed to magically keep refilling when he wasn't looking. He was doing good.

I stayed back wanting to give him that time. I

remembered my grandfather's party. I wanted to get lost in everything, in everyone. If only to forget the pain for a moment. Crow needed to forget.

It was also selfish because the kiss replayed in my mind over and over on a reel that wouldn't stop no matter how hard I tried.

This morning, I got up before him and fed Van, then helped her with her hair. When it was my turn, I took my time getting ready. When Crow got up, each of my moves were calculated to prevent the confrontation.

Today wasn't the day to deal with this. I wouldn't disrespect his loss, his grief, or his dad by putting more on Crow today. He had enough on his plate and hearing about how it hurt me that he kissed her wasn't on the menu.

Therefore, I'd done my part, sitting next to him at the service and giving him space.

Austyn, Bristyl, Carsyn, my mom and I all sat off to the side at a table and chairs, watching everything around us. My family was all driving back to Sumner after this, therefore they weren't drinking a whole lot. Princess was off with Goldi, knowing her for a long time and wanting to catch up.

My dad, Cruz, Cooper, Nox and Ryker were off talking to their brothers.

"Are you sure you want to go back tonight?" I asked the table, really not wanting them to. If they could just stay a couple of days that would be ideal. Maybe talking to them would get my head screwed on straight about what I saw. Then it came down to if I really wanted them to know.

Mom rolled her eyes. "You know your father. Wants to sleep in his own bed." I did know that, but that didn't mean that everyone else had to go.

"What about you guys?" I looked to Austyn and Bristyl.

"We're goin' back too," Austyn said. "I've got clients tomorrow at the salon, and Ryker has something goin' on."

Disappointment filled me more than I thought possible. It hadn't been long, but I missed them. Missed my family. Even more when my heart was cracked.

"Your father is pissed as hell you got on the back of that bike," my mother threw out there, and all I did was nod. "How long has this thing between you and Crow been going on?"

"Not long," I responded.

"Who's that?" Bristyl asked, interrupting the conversation, for which I was grateful for as I looked behind me.

Sophia was sidled up to Crow. His arm around her shoulder, her hand on his chest as she gazed up at him with so much love it physically hurt to witness. He laughed at something she said and then kissed the top of her head. My already cracked heart fractured wide.

Her expression beamed. Yeah. She loved him. What wasn't to love though. Crow was Crow. He was a great father, man, and companion.

What really hurt though, was the look on Crow's face as he talked to her. He was attentive and relaxed like they did this all the time in front of all his brothers, who I noted all knew her. Standing close like she was meant to be there.

The glint in his eyes sealed it though. I read that look, and I didn't like what I saw. But I was woman enough to understand it.

He loved her too.

Last night I didn't get to see that part because his back was to me. The only view I had was of Sophia, and she was in heaven. Seeing this, the way he loved her back, was a knife to the chest and soul. So much so it was bleeding.

"That's Sophia. Greer's mom." I rose from the table as the pain consumed me. Like gasoline to a flame, everything was burning up deep in my soul. "Need to pee. Be back." Taking off down the hallway, my throat gained a lump and wet threatened to spill from my eyes.

My nose tingled, and I knew it was coming. The bathroom was close and I just had to get to it, let myself have a moment and get my shit together. There was no crying in front of people. Fuck that. That gave the ones around you power, and that wouldn't happen with me.

I'd do it privately, just like last night and wash it away along with everything else.

"Rylynn!" the voice I recognized all too well called. Therefore, I sucked all the tears and sadness in and pushed it so far down it wouldn't show. It was hard, but I managed. Greer came my way.

This wasn't going to be good, I could feel it down to my bones.

"Yeah." My throat was crisp and clear, exactly like I intended.

He was as tall as me, and I was tall for a woman, no doubt going to be his father's height in a few years. Greer was Crow yet so much younger. He hadn't lived a rough life. His hands were too clean. It just meant that Sophia and Crow kept him that way. Which was good. It was what my family did for me, not letting the dregs of the earth hit me in any way.

"Know you saw my mom and dad."

That dagger twisted in my chest, but I didn't respond just continued to bleed.

"So you can see they love each other. You should leave before you get hurt. *They* always get hurt when it comes to my mom."

Keeping every feeling inside of me in check, I

listened but tightened my fists as the anger started swirling with the pain. Never a good combination.

"They were high school sweethearts. She always goes over to his house and spends the night with him." That thought had my stomach turning. Lord, please tell me he did not fuck me on sheets that he fucked her in. No. He wouldn't do that. Fuck, would he?

"They're going to get back together. They always do, and whoever he's with just flutters away. Hell, half those chicks out there he's been with. And you're like the rest of them. Better just go now before you really get hurt. We're a family, and you can't fuck that up."

He turned and walked down the hall. I darted into the bathroom and then the stall, locked the door and sat down. I really did have to pee, and while I was, everything that Greer said rolled around in my head. Of course, Crow loved her. Sophia gave him Greer, and it was plain as day how much he loved his son. I'd seen them kiss just yesterday, and as I laid in his bed last night I told myself I would talk to him. That I would find out what was going on. That I wouldn't go off half-cocked and not get answers from him.

But if he loved Sophia and she was here, in Rebellion, why would he have me jump on the back of his bike knowing that by bringing me here we'd be in the same air space, if he wanted to be with her. He knew the type of woman I was and knew that wouldn't fly.

Last night he asked me to stay with him, live with

him and start a life. That he wanted to try this with me and see where it went. I couldn't respond because I didn't trust it with the grief swirling around him. Then the kiss happened, and I still vowed to talk to him.

Today, he held my hand the entire time during the service, never once reaching for hers. Not that she was close enough for that, but still. Crow wrapped me in his arms for comfort.

I get that Greer wanted his parents together, but I didn't know if Crow wanted that. Hell, I didn't know a lot of things. But I'd talk to him. Another thing on the list of many I'd learned from my parents. Always talk.

Once the dust settled tomorrow, we'd sit and do just that. There were too many high emotions at play. While I didn't want to fuck that up, I also wouldn't be someone's side piece. I was never going to be some-one's second, and that needed to get cleared up with Crow.

Tomorrow we would talk. Sort this out and be on the same page.

After washing my hands, I left the bathroom and headed toward the bar, the resolve of my decision washing through me along with the relief of it. Funny how when you made up your mind about something that the situations become clearer. At least that was what it did for me. It was a new sense of resolve. We'd talk, and I'd find out the why. If he did love her, then I'd go home and this would be over.

Communication was always important, and we had to have that.

Coming out of the bathroom my resolve was to talk to him, hear him out, and go from there.

My feet stopped of their own will like tar was under them, heart fell to the floor, and soul shattered into a million pieces never to be put back together again. It was as if my insides were being ripped out piece by piece then put into a blender and disintegrated.

Sophia was up on her tiptoes, eyes closed and her lips were on Crow. The guys around him smiled like they were used to seeing this display of affection between the two of them. Like this was the norm. That... that was agony.

Crow's hand was in her hair as I watched in shock.

The brothers around him continued to smile as they watched.

Crow and Sophia pulled away, and he smiled down at her like he did to me yesterday. That communicated to me that he wanted to go further with our relationship. That he wanted us to be an us for real this time. But it was for her, not me.

Those were supposed to be my lips.

Those hands.

Those smiles.

He was supposed to be my man.

My heart. Yeah, I loved him, thinking that he could

be the one like my father was for my mother. The one who held me as I held him. The one that we worked together to get shit done each holding the other's heart and soul in their hands. Love just blew in my face.

It was all a front. He wasn't my end game. He was hers.

The tears wanted to fall, but I grasped on to the only thing that would stop them in their tracks. Anger. The one emotion that would stop the pain slicing through me. Because anger I could work with. The other shit needed to fly out the window, at least until I was alone and could let it out.

Crow wasn't mine.

He was hers. Always had been. Always would be.

Greer was right. As much as I hated to admit it, he was right. They were too public with their affections for it not to be. Crow wouldn't be kissing the woman in front of all his brothers if it wasn't real.

Maybe I was meant to be on the outside always looking in. Maybe my destiny was to wander through life unfulfilled. Maybe the fire inside of me, the one fueled by pain, was meant to burn bright while the longing would never be gone.

I had a thirst for life, for love, for family. I had it all.

In Sumner.

For a bit, I allowed my naivety to win. I allowed my stupid heart to believe the words he told me.

But when one drowning in pain had a taste of

peace, they would do anything to hold onto it... at least until they found a long-term way to dull the hurt.

I was a taste of peace for him.

A momentary comfort.

What we had wasn't real. I could see that with Sophia.

I looked over at my dad who was in a heated conversation and not paying attention. Neither were Cruz, Cooper, Nox or Ryker, who were involved with a game of pool.

At least there was that. Nothing like being completely humiliated in front of an entire club only to have it be in front of your family as well.

This meant though, that my time here was done. Not a single reason for me to stay.

Straightening my spine, I moved to the table I left earlier with my family. "Didn't Nox drive here in a GMC?"

The table all looked at each other. "Yeah, his bike had bad fuel. Had to flush the system, and he didn't want to deal with sputtering on the ride here so better safe than sorry. Why?" Austyn answered me. I needed to go and get as far away from Rebellion as I could. This game, I couldn't be a part of anymore. Twice he kissed her. Twice. With me in the same airspace. With my family here. What would happen when I wasn't here? Did he fuck her too? On the same bed sheets as me?

The second kiss changed everything. The talking portion of this relationship went flying out the window and landed in a pit of fire disintegrating into dust. He threw everything away. He disrespected me. Fuck it killed.

"Great. Can we leave?"

My mother's eyes widened in surprise. "I thought you were staying here."

I grabbed my mother's hand and squeezed letting her know with everything inside of me that I was hanging on by a thread and needed to get as far away from here as I could. "I need to go home. Can you please get me there?"

Mom's eyes searched my face then went over to Crow. Sophia was now standing next to him, gazing up and smiling, her hand on his arm. "Oh," Mom said, and it made me relax just a touch that she hadn't seen the kiss. From the looks of everyone else at the table, they didn't either.

"It's fine. I just want to go home." It was a partial lie, the fine part, and I hated doing it, but desperate times called for desperate measures. Any more time in this place and I'd either be destroyed or make sobbing sounds like a fool. Neither were an option.

"Maybe you should go and talk to him," Bristyl chipped in, leaning into the table. "I mean that's his kid's mom, so they're gonna be close."

"Just want to go home." She didn't see Crow and

Sophia's kiss either. She didn't feel the burn of it, and I wasn't going to add in that information. That would lead to my family getting pissed off, and that wasn't going to happen. If they knew what he did, their reaction would be a complete one-eighty.

Plus, it would make me feel like a bigger chump than I already felt. "I have some cases to work on."

That was true. The missing girl case was still ongoing. There were Penny and two boys that I needed to speak to and find out what they saw.

"Are you sure about this?" Carsyn, the quiet one, spoke up surprising me. She hadn't said much the entire time. "Maybe talking to him first would be best."

"I am going to talk to him and tell him that I'm going. I have a key to his house to get the stuff I bought." Come to think of it, he bought it because I had no cash on me. Therefore, it wasn't mine. Just like he wasn't mine. No way I'd keep any of that shit. "Never mind. I just want to go like this."

My mom could see it, and I didn't want her to. The way her face was getting soft, it couldn't happen. And if she caught on to everything, Austyn would be next. Thank God, Princess wasn't sitting here or I'd be fucked. That woman could read you by glancing at you. No bullshit there. A glance and you were fucked.

"Ry. This isn't good," Austyn said eyeing me. Yep, she was getting it.

I rose from my chair telling everyone it was time. I

had to find a quiet place to have the breakdown that needed to happen. "I'm going to tell him I'm leaving with you. I'd really, really appreciate it if you could get everyone ready to go and out the door on the double."

With deep sighs, my family broke off and spoke to their men. My father's glare on me was the hardest, and I just gave him a soft smile. We all started heading for the door, but pulling out everything I'd learned in Ravage, my strength was on high alert as I stopped next to Crow and Sophia.

Crow jolted when I touched his arm, like he forgot I was there at the clubhouse. Like I was a nuisance or one of the club mommas who shouldn't be touching him. Not like the woman who'd been sharing his bed.

That fucking killed. Invisible. That was exactly what I felt. Vapor. Nonexistent. Nothing.

Once bitten, twice shy. Fuck that.

Instead of crying, I held onto the anger and plastered on a wide smile. "Sorry to interrupt." Not really, but I was rolling with it. Hell, I couldn't even muster up a smartass comment. But I guessed that was what happened when your heart no longer existed because it'd been burned to ash. "I'm taking off with my family and just wanted to say bye."

Looking up at Crow, his eyes blinked a couple of times, something working behind them, then his face appeared stricken, turning hard to Sophia then to me. "What?" he bit off, turning his back to Sophia who I didn't dare look at. There was no need for her to know that I saw them. That seeing it broke something inside of me. Something that was never given to anyone before. It would just give her more ammunition. Hell, she'd probably pull him in for another kiss right in front of me to put salt in the wound. If that happened, she'd be in for a very rude awakening. Member or not, I was Ravage, and we didn't put up with that shit.

Raising my chin, I fired, "I'm going home with my family. I'm really sorry about your dad. Thank you for having me." *Thank you for having me? Seriously Ry, what the fuck was that?*

He glowered. "You're not leaving."

He came toward me, but I took a step back. A hard arm wrapped around my chest and judging from the tattoos, it was my father. I closed my eyes, not wanting whatever this to happen. My father was already pissed. We didn't need this added into it. "She wants to go. She's goin'," my father growled, pulling me out of the clubhouse with Crow on our heels.

I tried dragging my feet to get my father to stop, which I didn't understand why I did, but he just picked me up higher so I wasn't touching the ground. He placed me next to Nox's SUV, and Crow was there. Pissed as all hell. Fury all over him like I'd never seen before.

Even with the anger I felt, there was no energy to fight what was happening here. He didn't love me and the sooner I came to terms with that, the better off my heart would be.

I'd remembered everything Greer told me and my decision to hear him out. I remembered hotel sex, eating pizza out of a box, him needing me, greeting everyone who came to his home, him asking me to stay with him in Rebellion. The feelings for me that I swore I saw in his eyes.

Then I remembered the first kiss between him and his true love, I witnessed when I wasn't supposed to. Then the one in front of all his brothers, my family seconds from seeing.

Fuck, it tore at me. Never knew pain like this before. It was very similar to the death of a loved one. Having them ripped out of your life and learning what your new normal would be without them.

I'd have to do the same thing when it came to Crow.

He'd no longer exist for me. My nose started to burn, and throat began to close.

I let my pain connect with his. I let passion fuel our fire.

What I didn't do was use my head. What I didn't do was guard my heart.

Shame on me.

Fool me once, shit happens.

I was Rylynn Hutton, and I wouldn't get fooled again.

I was the firstborn daughter to Rhys Hutton and tough as they came.

Swallowing down my anger, my betrayal, my hurt, I took in everything. All the emotions, I let them well up inside me and then I took one deep, long breath.

Push that shit down to the very depths of my soul. Get through until I could get back to reality.

Once upon a time, I believed in fairy tales.

Then life kicked me in the teeth.

Once upon a time, I believed I could have love.

Then I felt the realities of a broken heart.

Once upon a time, I would have done anything for the man they called Crow.

That all vanished in a doorway with a single kiss.

And in that very moment, I made a vow to myself. A vow to my pain.

No one would ever see me hurt, no one would ever feel my heart. And no one would have me again.

Keeping my smile on my face and even with my father next to me, I looked up at Crow, anger pouring out of him, and I had no idea what was in mine. What I felt was devastation. Pain. Agony. Death. Heartbreak.

But in the end, this was what was best. He could be with Sophia and Greer. Add in little Van, they had their ready-made family.

I walked to Crow knowing this would be the last time I ever saw him again. Knowing that even if I did see him again, I would turn and go the other way.

Knowing that I loved him in a way that would never be forgotten until I took my last breath. He held my heart and didn't even know it. He'd also crushed it.

Every thought seared into me like a brand burning my soul and scarring it for life. They would never heal. They would be there for whatever life threw at me for the years to come. The marks would become pieces of me, and over time I'd deal. It was what life was. A series of ups and downs that developed a person stronger than the day before.

It wasn't the time to bring up the kisses and throw them in his face. As much as I itched too, that wouldn't happen. I didn't want his last memory of me to be me bitching and screaming at him. Even if he tore my heart out, that wasn't how I wanted to go out. I had too much pride in myself for it.

Maybe if I'd have said yes to him about staying right away, he wouldn't have kissed another woman. I didn't know the answer to that and the could've, would've, should've was a dangerous game. That I knew, but it was hard not to think.

Holding everything in, I clutched on to his hands holding them between us, feeling how rough and strong his were, remembering how they felt on my body. "You are a wonderful man, Crow. When you let someone in, you're the most caring man I've met. You go all in, and I've felt it. I felt you." Shit, this was hard. My hands started to shake, but I couldn't stop them.

"But this is where our paths go different ways. You have a family in there who loves you. Let them in and love them back. Be happy, Crow. Your dad would want that for you."

"What are you talking about, Ry? This isn't..."

I lifted up and kissed his lips a final time, putting every bit of what I was feeling into it. Telling him without words how much I loved him and how hurt I was that he didn't feel the same way because if he did, those kisses would've never happened.

Thoughts of moments ago when another woman's lips were in the same place, it came crashing down on me once more. Rolling down I stepped out of his grasp as he lunged for me, but my father got in his way.

"Dad. Don't." The tone must've cut through to him, to both of them because they stopped. "I don't want this."

"Why are you leaving, Ry? This makes no sense."

Giving him the best smile I could, I said, "So you can be with your family." Only then did I get in the SUV, and Nox took off out of the gate.

I didn't look back because I knew if I did, I'd want to run into his arms. That wasn't an option anymore. He wasn't mine. No matter how much I willed it to be different, it didn't work. I'd never be considered second best. I deserved a man who put me first. And Crow didn't. It was disrespectful of him to kiss her at his home. It was a thousand times worse to do it in his club with all his brothers around, when they knew I'd been at his place the last few days playing hostess.

I'd seen love between two people. How it grew and changed over the years. Even how knowing someone your whole life turned into the one you were meant to be with. All of it I'd either seen or been told with the stories of how the Ravage MC ol' ladies found their men.

Crow needed his time with Sophia to work out whatever was going on between them. They loved each other. Had a kid together. I wasn't a part of that and never would be.

Never knew how much heartbreak could hurt. To know the man you loved, loved someone else. I didn't know how much it would tear at your insides, scaring you for life. Never knew that letting something go would mean losing yourself in the process.

Only after we got out of Rebellion did I allow the tears to fall freely down my cheeks.

And I did it the entire way back to Sumner.

CHAPTER ELEVEN
Crow

"KEVIN, MAKE IT GONE."

There was no hesitation in his voice, but considering we were on the phone and not in person, he couldn't tell my current mood, which was deteriorating fast. Fuck, it hadn't gotten any better since last night, and this fucker was on my last nerve. "I'm on it. I'll have it done."

"You'd better." I hung up the phone, frustration building. Who the fuck was I kidding. I was already there ready to rip someone's fucking head off.

Waking up this morning in the fucking safe room at the club just started the day off as shit. I was too drunk last night to go after Rylynn, and my brothers had to lock me down. That I was also pissed about.

"Brother!" Brewer called as I got on my bike, ready to take off and follow Rylynn. My step faltered. I knew I'd

drank a lot, but didn't think I was drunk. My head felt a bit off though. It was stupid to get on my bike, but I didn't give a fuck.

Something was seriously wrong with this entire situation, and we needed to talk this out. She couldn't go back to Sumner. She wasn't going to give up on us.

Brewer, Wrong Way, Tex, Hornet and Rooster all ran up in front of my bike blocking me in.

"I'll run you the fuck over. Get out of my way."

"Sorry, brother, can't let you do that," Wrong Way said as I glared at him.

"Let me?" I ground out. "I'm the motherfuckin' president of this club. You'll move out of my fuckin' way!"

They each looked at one another, and I'd thought they'd given in. Except they didn't. All as one they descended on me, my bike crashing to the ground. Pissed wasn't even the word for it. Livid. Punches were thrown and between all of them, they got me under control, but not my mouth.

"Let me the fuck go now!" I yelled as my brothers got me in the clubhouse and down the stairs. "You fuckin' lock me in there, you'll fuckin' pay," I growled, seeing the safe room next to my office in the basement's door, wide and ready for someone to enter. It was a padded room with cameras on the inside. A bed and sink was there for any guests. It didn't get used much, but apparently, that was where they were going to try to lock me up.

I'd fought. They won.

The next thing I remembered was waking up in

that fucking place. The walls were too white and the room to fucking small. Confinement wasn't my thing. These fuckers knew it, but they were doing me a solid even if I fucking hated it.

Unlucky for Ethan, he was the first one I saw and laid him out with one punch to the eye. I was pissed at my brothers for it. Would be for a while, but took it out on Ethan immediately. The others stayed away, and I kept the door shut on my office not needing anyone's shit.

They were all still going to hear from me.

Later that afternoon, there was surprisingly a knock at the door. Wonder who had the balls to come in here with me. Whoever it was had brass ones.

"What?"

The door swung open and Brewer stepped in, a gash above his eye and bruise on his jaw. Good. "Pissed?" he asked, lifting his brow and already knowing the fucking answer.

My already hot temper flared, ready to add to his cuts and bruises. "What do you think? Come close enough and I'll fuckin' show ya," I challenged, wanting him to take me up on it.

"Will it help?"

This caught me as strange and made me pause. "What?"

He stepped forward proud as can be. "If you want to punch me... more. Do it. Get that shit out and get over it. It's not gonna make any of the shit that happened last night go away."

Fuck, the man was right. Hated that, but I still wanted to beat the fuck out of someone. I'd been trying to get my head on straight since I woke up and sort the shit with Rylynn out. It hadn't gone well. There was nothing I could remember as to why she'd jump in the car with Nox and take off. Nor the tears she tried to hide that threatened to burst from her eyes.

"You goin' after her?" he asked.

Not many men would call me out on something, but Brewer was the exception. Growing up together, he had more pull than I probably should let him. He wasn't afraid to lay the reality at my feet and make me hear him. Didn't mean that I didn't want to shut his mouth up. I stayed silent because there wasn't an answer to that yet. My mind was a jumble of thoughts pissing me off.

He sat in the chair in front of me crossing his foot over his knee. "You know we couldn't let you go drunk last night. As much as you're pissed, you know we did what we had to."

"Fuck." I rubbed my hands over my face. They had my back, and I beat the shit out of them. I wanted to continue to beat the shit out of them. It was a combination of everything though. It was all riding on me hard.

"Right. Now that counseling time is over, let's get to

business. We need to take a ride to Stagnet. The Purple Pride."

"Thought Tex and Phoenix went there and it was a bar. More than that?"

"Yeah. Tommy came through and called Wrong Way." My gaze turned stormy as Brewer continued, "You were goin' through shit, and I'd have been pissed he called you about that shit."

That didn't make me feel better. I just nodded.

"A holding company, Wicked Industries, owns the Purple Pride."

"This means nothing to me," I clipped.

Brewer reached in his cut and pulled out a sheet of paper handing it over to me. "Apparently Ebony owns the place."

"You're fuckin' shittin' me." I took the paper and began to read. Sure as shit, her name was the executor of the company.

He shook his head. "Nope."

"Where'd you get this?"

Brewer leaned back in his seat. "The info, Tommy. The sheet in your hand, Wrong Way cracked into the lawyer's server and pulled it up."

"Where was Lemon?"

Brewer shook his head. "Fuck if I know."

Lemon was getting further and further on my shit list. He'd better hope not to see me today or a bullet could find its way into his head.

"We need a ride to the Purple Pride and then see if we can find Ebony and find out what the fuck is going on."

"Get everyone rounded up." It was time for some fucking answers.

Brewer held up his hand catching my attention. "Got Carlo's replacement here. You gonna tear him apart I bring him in here?

"Possibly."

Brewer chuckled. "This'll be one thing done and out of the fuckin' way." He left the room. This wasn't what I wanted to do today, but it was my job. As pissed as I was, it needed done.

A knock came to the door, and it opened. Brewer walked in and behind him was a man in his forties or fifties. Tattoos on his arms with a buzz cut. Face steel. Interesting. Rising from the chair, I held my hand out. "Crow."

"Tony." He took my hand, and it was strong. Another good thing.

"Sit."

Brewer started naming shit off to tell me how qualified the guy was. I held my hand up, and he stopped. Leaning into my desk, I put my elbows on top and looked Tony straight in the eye.

"You know who we are?"

"Yes," he answered immediately.

"You know if you fuck us, we'll fuck you."

"Yes."

"That means a bullet in your head." He didn't flinch. "You do the job and get paid. You get us the information we need. Wrong Way will be in charge of the place, and you're under him. You fuck up. He tells me, and I handle it. Is that clear?"

His focus never left me. It was impressive. "Yes."

"Don't piss me off," I told him, nodding to Brewer. "Head out."

Brewer took the man out.

I picked up my phone and dialed Rylynn. Once again. She didn't answer.

NEEDING to be on my bike, the ride to Stagnet was good. Even with my mind on Rylynn and the reason for the ride, the sun and wind felt reassuring. Bear stayed at the club while the rest of us rolled out.

We cut our engines right outside the Purple Pride. The building itself was small, white outside with beer logo signs in the windows. It looked like an old house renovated to be a bar. Behind it was a very large barn, one that looked like it'd been there for years, but had a brand new paint job.

Tire tracks led to the large door on the left side.

Before we swung our legs off our bikes, the small

side door of the barn opened and several men walked out. Their guns weren't out, but could be seen. They were locked and loaded, making me wonder what the fuck was in that building.

Getting off quick, we didn't have to walk to them. They came to us instead.

"No reason for you to be out here," the one obviously in the lead declared. He was clean cut with dark hair. Jeans, shirt, nothing out of the ordinary.

He had about a dozen men at his back.

It wasn't him that caught my attention though. It was Simon, Sophia's man, that was in the middle of the group that did. His face was stone, either he didn't recognize me or he did and didn't give a fuck.

"We just came up for a beer. This is a bar, isn't it?" I asked seeing some cars parked in front of the bar. "Heard of this place and wanted to check it out. Is there a problem?"

"You're not welcome here."

"Right," I said, wondering why Tex and Phoenix didn't get this nice welcome when they stopped up here. "Why is that? Is there somethin' that Ravage needs to know about up here?"

"Nothin' that's any of your business," another man, this one blond, said with his arms crossed his chest. He was short yet stocky.

"You mean to tell me we hauled our asses all the

way up here for nothin'," Wrong Way said at my side. "I wanted a beer."

The blond reached, and I whipped out my gun aiming it at him. All guns from both sides went up quick. Each side facing the end of a chamber ready to have a bullet put in their heads.

"You runnin' drugs, guns, or pussy?" I asked like it was a normal conversation to have over a dozen guns pointed at my head. It'd been awhile since we had any issues, but once they came, they decided to come all at the same time.

"None of your fuckin' business."

Phoenix took a step forward. "Everything in and around Rebellion is our business. But you know that, and you're still trying to do fucked up shit. You think we wouldn't come for you?"

"We don't give a fuck who you think you are. We know who we are, and we protect what's ours," the dark-haired man replied, not even a wobble to his gun. Impressive. These guys were trained either from years of doing this or some kind of military background.

"Seems like we have at least one thing in common. Ebony own this place?" I asked.

A few eyes went to others, and the two in the very back were the weak ones. One was visibly sweating, it pouring down his face. The other's gun hand was shaking and eyes were wired. Those would be the two we needed for answers. The rest of these fucks it would be more difficult. Not impossible, we just went the path of least resistance.

I shrugged when no one answered. "No worries. We'll go visit her."

They said nothing as we put our weapons away, got on our bikes, and rode for a while, then pulled over to a clearing off the side of the road. We needed to brief about what just happened in there.

Standing under the tree, I spoke, "Alright. First thing is first. Sophia's man, Simon, was there. Dark hair in the middle." I looked at Wrong Way. "You call Ethan and my boy. You get all that asshole's stuff out of Sophia's house in the next two hours along with a new code for her alarm and new locks. Ethan stays outside that house. If that fucker comes around, you tell him to blow his fuckin' head off. I'll deal with it."

Wrong Way nodded, and I turned to the guys. "What are we thinkin' here? It's out in the middle of nowhere, so I'm not thinkin' pussy. I'm thinkin' they're cookin'."

Nods came while Hornet spoke, "That or they have a distribution center there. Either drugs or guns. Did you see what they were packin'. That's pretty hard artillery to have, and if they're dealin' guns we got a bigger fuckin' problem."

Brewer added, "And we need to get it locked down as soon as possible or this shit will get ugly."

Looking to Hornet and Rooster, I said, "Need eyes

inside that place. What will it take to get them there?"

Hornet huffed out a huge breath. "Fuck if I know. I know we can't get in the place unless it's a time when no one's there, but since we showed up they'll be more vigilant. I'll see what I can come up with."

"The two guys in the back. The one sweatin' and the one shakin'. Did you see 'em?" I asked everyone.

"Yeah," came from Wrong Way, and a "yes," came from Brewer.

"We need those two. Don't care how the fuck you get them, but we need them and any information we can drag up. Those are the weak links."

Tex nodded along with several others.

"Tex and Wrong Way, on that shit and report back."

"Got it," they said at the same time.

"I'll run by Ebony's again and see if she's there," Phoenix said.

"Fine, but you take Lemon." They nodded, but Lemon hadn't looked me in the fuckin' eye since I saw him. Hiding something or know he's going to get his ass handed to him. That's the question.

"Right. Back to the clubhouse and get more information. Don't give a shit how you need to get it. Get it. We gotta get this shit sorted and do it now. Get Tommy's ass on this shit as well."

That and I needed to get a fucking hold of Rylynn.

Guess when things get fucked they just keep getting worse.

CHAPTER TWELVE
Rylynn

THE LAST FEW DAYS I'D BEEN NOTHING BUT MISERABLE. Learning you actually loved someone and they didn't feel the same hurt beyond measure. It was a physical pain in the chest knowing that the man you'd love to be next to didn't want you there.

I'd felt it each mile I rode away from him in Rebellion. It was what needed to be done though. He loved her. As much as it killed what Crow did, Greer was right. They would get back together and be a family.

Witnessed it with my own eyes. Twice.

Fool me once, shame on you.

Fool me twice, shame on me.

I was no fucking fool.

A hard pounding came to the door. It was my father, could tell by the sound. It was his calling card.

At least it gave me a few moments to pull my shit together before he would barge in and grill me.

He'd allowed me to keep to myself for a while, which I appreciated, but knew my time was coming to an end. I was actually surprised that it took this long. My father wasn't a patient man. It said a lot about him, giving me the time to get my head screwed on. I could use a lot longer though to get right about Crow.

Getting up I moved to the door, seeing my father through the peephole and opening it up. "Hey, Daddy dearest."

He wrapped his arms around me hugging me tight. Not realizing the comfort was much needed, I melted into my father pulling from his strength, soaking in every drop. I hated feeling weak in any way, but fuck if this didn't cut me to the quick. He didn't move for long moments giving me his time. That was him though. He always gave his girls everything. Even when he was pissed at us, he always gave. He was that kind of dad. Hell, he was that kind of man. Loved him with everything inside of me, and no one would fault me for wanting that for myself.

Crow just wasn't that guy.

Dad pulled away and went to my couch tossing his big, beefy body down. I swore I heard the springs creak in protest. Sitting next to him on the opposite end, I came right out with it. My dad didn't pussyfoot around shit and neither did I. "Crow and I were together a couple of times. He was hurting, and I cared about him. So I got on his bike and went to Rebellion. It's no big deal, and it's over."

"Why?" my father asked as my head whipped to him, not expecting that question at all. I'd thought he'd be happy it was over, not asking me why. That was unusual for him.

"Why what?"

"Why's it over?" he grunted in the way only he could.

Well, that surprised me. I expected him to ask why I got on the bike and took off leaving my family and everything I knew behind. He'd understand that I cared about the man, but he'd want to get down to the nitty gritty of it. Instead, he wanted to know why it was over.

Pulling my knees up, my arms went around them tight. My father would wait the few beats it took me to pull my words together. He'd done it so many times when I was little, waiting until I came clean about something and always getting it out of me one way or the other. He was creative in his ways.

Therefore, instead of procrastinating I talked. "He needs to be with his family."

"Explain," he demanded, snaking chills up my arms.

"He's got a son and daughter. He has deep feelings for his boy's mom, and she loves him too. They should be together for their kid." I left out the part about them kissing, especially considering Crow was Cruz's kid. All of that was some jacked up shit.

Dad leaned forward coming closer to me, and I swore he smelled my bullshit. "Just because someone has a kid with a woman doesn't mean they're gonna be together. You're smarter than that shit."

That pissed me right the hell off because I was smart and didn't just come up with this shit out of the blue. I wanted to talk, I just didn't get to that because his actions changed my mind. My foot went down on the floor, while my other came up on the couch bending at the knee so I was turned to my father, blood pumping through my veins rapidly as the anger took over.

"That's exactly what I thought. Just because he has a kid means shit. Then, I saw him kissing his boy's mother the night before the funeral. Let it go so we could talk about it after all the shit of the day was done. When his boy found me at the clubhouse and spewed all kinds of stupid shit, I knew it was exactly that because he wanted his mom and dad together. The more he spewed, the more I didn't give a shit. I was going to talk to Crow as soon as I could and get every-thing ironed out. I mean, maybe it was a fluke with the kiss. Hell if I knew, but I was going to give him the benefit of the doubt. Then I come out of the bathroom at the clubhouse and Sophia is up on her tiptoes, head up and Crow's got his down. They were kissing, again."

This visions of them together blasted my head, and I couldn't turn it off. Living in my head wasn't the way to go, but I'd been doing it for days unable to talk about it.

I stood up in my living room and started to pace needing the movement. I hadn't talked about any of this, and here I was—with my father of all people— pouring everything out and knowing it wouldn't be good, but needing it out of me. My father didn't do well with anyone hurting his girls, but I wasn't stupid and he needed to know that as well. This decision wasn't made on a whim.

"He kissed her, with me there twice. The first time, he didn't know I saw because I was in the hallway of his house and went right to bed so I didn't have to talk about it, with it being his father's funeral the next day and all. Then when I went up to him to tell him I was leaving the clubhouse after the second kiss. He jumped, obviously forgetting I was there and not realizing I saw him again. Since I wasn't a priority for him, I left. End of discussion."

"Good," my father said, halting my feet as I spun to him.

"What do you mean good?"

He leaned back in the couch putting his arm up

along the back. "Not only did he kiss some piece, he's not good enough."

"He's your brother and the president of his charter. How is that not good enough?" I asked, coming closer, my arms now crossed over my chest. The urge to defend Crow hit me like a pile of bricks, and it was fierce. I hated it, but couldn't stop it either.

"First, he let you go."

I sat back in the couch. "What?"

"He let you go, Ry. You told him you were leavin' and he let you. Not good enough for you."

Tears pricked the back of my eyes. He was right, but... that didn't mean I was off the hook too. "I didn't give him an option."

My father leaned in. "You don't think I would fight to the death to get through someone or something to get to your mom? That right there is a man who's good enough for my daughter. Until that time, fuck 'em."

"What's the second?" I asked cautiously.

"Been around the block. Know the woman was his kid's mom, but if he was into you and only into you, he wouldn't have put his lips on anyone else. You see me goin' around kissin' the bitches around here?"

"No."

"Right. So not good enough."

Giving up, I moved next to my father and curled in a ball against him. Silent tears fell onto my shirt as my father wrapped his arms around me. "Get from the tears you liked 'em."

"I fell for him, Dad, and did it hard. Didn't realize how much until I rode away from Rebellion." No way was I telling my father that I loved him. No way, no how. That would make my father's anger worse, but he was here and obviously it needed to get off my chest.

"Then I'm glad he's a state over. You don't need that shit." He kissed the top of my head. "My girl deserves the best."

He was right, I did deserve the best. And I would find it. When I found the man for me, I would be the number one in his life, not a runner-up prize or second best. Instead of laying myself out there for a man, he should be laying out his shit for me. Crow didn't do that.

"You mean to tell me you have no idea what happened that night?" The pimpled kid sat on the couch, his mom and dad surrounding him on both sides. Today was as good a day as any to dig deeper into Elizabeth's case. Add in I needed something to get my mind off Crow and this was the perfect distraction.

Hell, I'd scrub the bathrooms in the clubhouse if it

would give me a reprieve. Now that was saying something because those things were fucking gross.

Irwin, the kid, shook his head over and over again as he darted his eyes to his parents. While having them gone would be best, he was underage and I wasn't stupid. Maybe a bit shocked that they even allowed it in the first place. Not being a cop didn't seem to matter much to them.

Holding up my phone, the screen showed Irwin and his friend, Snider, with Elizabeth. Then she disappeared and they were seen outside the door. "Is that you?"

"Yeah. But I don't know what happened. She smiled at us, and Sni thought maybe she liked him and went after her. I followed, but she never came out. Her friend Penny came to the door, knocked on it, but Elizabeth didn't answer. We took off."

That account goes hand in hand with what happened on the video. Not to mention Sni was a much cooler name than Snider. No wonder he changed it. "You didn't see anything or hear anything when she was in the bathroom?"

"I didn't hear anything, but the music was pretty loud."

"I think this is done," his father said, standing up from the couch where he and his wife flanked their son.

The boy turned to him, relief coming over his face.

His mother must've seen it because she said, "Tell her the truth."

"Mary!" the father exclaimed as he shot daggers at his wife.

"Don't you Mary me. This girl has been missing a long time. I couldn't imagine what that mother is going through. Answer her," she demanded once again.

Irwin shook his head once again. "Sni had his ear up to the door and was smilin'. He said he heard her flush the toilet, and I found it weird that something like that would make him happy. He said he heard some kind of racket then nothing. He pulled away, and we took off."

Paying a trip to Sni was my next go. "Thank you for your help."

The mother jumped up coming to the door to open it. "I hope you find that little girl," she said as I bid farewell and headed to the next one.

The trip to Sni's house was short.

When I pulled up to the house, all was quiet. No cars or windows open. Knocking on the door gave me more of nothing. Curtains were closed as well.

Looking at my watch, another cheating husband was on the agenda and meeting his piece at X. Studio X was a strip club run by Princess and owned by the club. This should be an easy go.

Anything to get my mind away from *him*.

CHAPTER THIRTEEN
Crow

SITTING IN CHURCH, I LOOKED AROUND THE TABLE AT MY brothers, all eager for answers that hopefully one of us had.

"Kevin knows too much. He needs to be dealt with," Phoenix said my thoughts out loud. Kevin had nothing for us on Rook's case and was becoming a liability to the club. One we didn't need. I'd called him twice getting the same roll around. The club was done with his shit.

"We all good with replacin' Kevin?" The vote went around the table.

I looked at Wrong Way. "Find a new lawyer. And make sure he knows what he's signing up for."

"On it."

"What do we do about Kevin?" Phoenix asked with a devilish smirk. "I want him dead."

"Agreed," I said then continued. "Let's put it on hold for right now. Keep him on as Rook's lawyer so we can keep eyes on him. That way when all this other shit pans out, we can deal with him."

The table nodded in understanding. It was the best thing for the club at the moment.

"Ebony? Anyone find her?"

A loud banging came on the church door. Everyone around here knew when those doors were closed no one knocked or bothered us unless it was serious shit, like the fucking place getting blown up. Nodding at Phoenix, he went to the door. Ethan was there. "I didn't knock, but..."

"Crow, get your ass out here right now." It was Sophia. I didn't mark talking to her about Simon being out of her house on my list of shit to get done. While it pissed me off she was interrupting church, I needed to give her time.

"Give me five," I told the guys, walking out of the room and closing the doors behind me.

"Sorry. She was comin' no matter what," Ethan started, and I just held up my hand to get him to shut the fuck up.

"Leave," I ordered him as he scurried off.

"I cannot believe you!" Sophia, not acting like Sophia yelled at me. We'd known each other forever and not once had she ever done that. Normally, she was calm, cool, and collected. One of the things I admired about her. She wasn't giving that to me currently.

"What the fuck is goin' on with you?"

"Oh, I don't know. You kicking my boyfriend out of my house without talking to me maybe." Her hands went to her hips in bitch pose. Yeah. This was unusual for Sophia.

"Get that, but this isn't like you."

Her eyes flared in a way I hadn't seen before. "This is me, Crow. You do not get to come into my life when you want and dictate what I do. Did I say a word about the little tart you had here for your father's funeral? So what makes you think you can tell me when I'm done with a relationship."

One word stuck out of all of that. "Tart?"

Her hands went up in the air. "Out of all of that, that's what you picked out?"

"Look, I should've come and talked to you, but shit's been crazy around here. The guy is bad news. Really bad news, just found that out. You need to stay away from him, and you need to keep my boy away from him."

"Bad news and what, you're good news?"

To say I was shocked would be an understatement of the year. Sophia was so even-keeled in all the years that I'd known her, she'd never acted like this. It was as if she wasn't in her own body or something.

"Tell me what's really goin' on here."

"What's he into?" she asked me instead of answering.

"Can't tell you that." One, because I didn't know and two, because it was club business.

"Of course you can't." She turned around and looked down at her shoes. I moved to her and put my hands on her arms. She sucked in a deep breath and said, "You kissed me."

"What? No, you kissed me."

"At your house, yeah. But at the clubhouse that night after the funeral, you kissed me."

Liquor was a dangerous concoction, and I had the slither go up my spine. Parts of that night were a bit fuzzy which was unlike me. Fuck. Please tell me I didn't do that shit. That couldn't have happened. "What?"

"Just forget it." She started to make her way out of the clubhouse when I got in front of her.

"Simon is a bad guy, and I wanted him away from you and my boy. I had other shit goin' on, so I'm sorry I didn't call and tell you. But where is all this other shit coming from?"

She turned around and looked up at me, those eyes that I'd loved at one time and still cared deeply about scoring at me. "One thing your father wanted was for us to be a family again. I thought with you kissing me in front of the club, your brothers, that's what was happening. Then with you kicking Simon out, I thought you wanted to be with me and wanted the man out of my life. I'm guessing this was a mistake. I came here so I could tell you unless you're comin' back to me, you don't get to dictate my life like movin' my boyfriend out of my house."

Fuck, she still loved me. After sixteen plus years, she still wanted me.

Sad thing was I loved her as my son's mother, not as someone who I wanted to spend my days with. This shit right here could fuck up a lot of things, and even treading lightly wouldn't help one bit. And all I could think about was if Rylynn saw me kiss Sophia and that was why she left. Fuck.

One thing at a time.

"I was drunk, Sophia. Memories are foggy. Sorry I kissed you and made you think that. But, babe, we've been over for a long time. You didn't want anything to do with the MC life, and I gave you that out. Remember?"

Her eyes beamed up at me. "What if I've changed my mind?"

If she would've told me this sixteen years ago, she'd have a ring on her finger and we'd be together. It was something I so badly wanted at the time. Sophia though, wanted me to give up the club, and that wasn't happening. She knew it going in but thought she'd change me. No one fucking changed me. I was who I was. The end.

The long huff of air that expelled from me didn't help a single fucking bit. "I'm not where you are, Soph. Not sayin' this to be a dick, just givin' it to ya straight. You're my kid's mom, and that's all you'll ever be to me."

"She left though," Sophia whispered.

Like I didn't fucking know that one. "Yeah."

"Are you bringing her back?" she asked with hope beaming from her.

"That's none of your business, Sophia."

"But it's your business to kick my boyfriend out of my house? You can't have things both ways, Crow."

That was when I did something that I'd never done with Sophia before. Never had to. I got into her space, her eyes widening. "You wanna be with that dickhead. Fine. But Greer comes and lives with me. You want that fuckup to mess up the life you've built, that's on you, but my boy does not live there with him. We've had a great relationship over the years, Soph, and I don't want to fuck that up, but this," I pointed between the two of us, "isn't happening. You've had more than your fair share of shots to get exactly what you wanted, and you never took one. Pushed me away. Then I bring home Rylynn and everything for you changes."

"She's a kid, Crow," Sophia responded.

"If you would've talked to her, you'd know differently." I stepped back. "You decide if you want to stay with that asshole. If it's yes, I expect my boy at my house. If he's not and I find out, I'll be over."

"You can't..." she started, but I'd already opened the doors to church, went inside, and shut them hard.

"She break your cock off?" Phoenix asked.

"You wanna suck it and see?" I retorted, falling down into my chair. This was fucked up. I now knew why Rylynn left, and it was all my fucking fault.

"What else do we need to talk about?" I questioned Brewer, not letting anyone get anymore jabs in.

"Tony's at the store. He and Gus are gettin' to know each other. Gus is on call to let us know if anything's amiss."

"Alright."

Hornet spoke up. "I've got eyes inside the building."

"How?" I asked, sitting up in my seat.

"Cat. Put a camera on her collar. The problem is she doesn't go to the places I need her to, but I'm workin' on that."

"Good. Where we at with Ebony?"

Wrong Way spoke up, "Searched her credit cards and she is, in fact, in North Carolina."

"Fuck. What else?" My eyes went to Lemon who put his head down. Fucker needed to be doing the searches.

"Just the eyes Tommy said. Don't know if that shit's real."

"We keep it real until we know it's not. That way our shit is covered. What about the guns?"

"Wells is set. We just need to set up a time for the drop." This was good. If we did have these fucking eyes, we needed to get the shit moved.

"Good. Buyer for the others?" I asked and watched his face closely. I knew it before he said it just from his expression.

"Just Starling." He paused waiting for me.

"Know that shit's a lot of cake, but we can't sell to them. They'll turn around and stab us in the back with our own shit. Even with a deal in place, there's no trust there and they'll break it. For me it's off the table." This was said with a finality that Brewer didn't miss as he nodded, then I continued, "When we move the hands, we take the AKs and ARs with us. We need to find a place to store them that prying eyes won't know about."

"Right. I'll get on setting all of that up."

I nodded, just needing this shit to be done. There was so much coming at me from all angles, and already being pissed about Rylynn didn't help one bit.

"That Damien Curtis from Xavier and Marcus's run. Xavier was right. He's made several moves on their territory, and Xavier's crew is holding their own for now. But here's the kicker," Brewer said while my imagination went crazy. "Damien called me and wanted to set up a meeting. Wants to move our business from Xavier to him. Told him I'd get back to him."

"Money talks. We have no allegiance to anyone," Wrong Way said. "Say we talk to them, give them a price that's off the charts high and see if they bite for it."

"Vote it," I called out, hearing the 'yeahs'. I slammed the gavel down looking at Brewer. "Make the call and set it up."

"On it."

"One more thing," I said to the table. "Talked to Wrong Way about patchin' in Ethan. Next church we vote. This is your heads up."

Walking out of the clubhouse, I headed home, needing a shower and shut-eye.

The call to Rylynn went unanswered once again. This was going to change.

Add this day to the many that were fucked up before.

"DADDY, WHAT'S WRONG?" my daughter asked while we ate dinner. Gourmet chef, fuck no. Put meat on a grill and make mac and cheese out of a box, fuck yeah.

That was a loaded question. Everything felt like chaos without Rylynn here. Pissed wasn't even the word for it. When she left anger took over me. Two seconds more and I would've punched Rhys to get to her, but the car she was in pulled out into the road and was gone.

Rhys just shook his head at me, went to his bike then he and Tanner took off. They all took off, and I was so pissed I didn't say good-bye to my new *family*.

Now come to find out, I set all that in play by my drunk antics. Fuck. Rylynn must be feeling this shit hard, and I couldn't blame her one bit. It was my fucking fault.

"Just miss your grandpa." It wasn't a lie fully. He just wasn't the only one I missed.

"Yeah. I do too." She picked at her mac and cheese going for her drink. "Mommy liked him."

One topic not up for discussion was her mother. Dealing with her was never an option. Hadn't heard from her since the funeral. Lemon had cameras on the house and she hadn't tried to get back in there. Who knew where the fuck she ended up. "Yeah. I know."

"Mommy probably needs me."

This killed me. A ten-year-old taking care of a thirty-year-old who had so many fucking drugs in her veins she couldn't make it to the toilet to puke. She'd been around that dysfunction long enough. I'd let it go on for too long. That was on my shoulders.

"You do a great job with her, Van. But it's time for her to take care of herself."

"What?"

While this choice wasn't hers, she would do it in a heartbeat. I'd always been open with my kids, and Van already knew how bad it could get. She'd seen more than she should. Therefore, I only added a bit of sugar to coat the sting. "Mommy is a grown-up, and she's sick. She went to a place to make her better, but she left. Right now there's nothing that you or I can do for her. We need to let her figure this out on her own."

"Why?"

"Why does she need to do it herself?" I asked as she nodded.

"Grown-ups need to be able to take care of themselves. They get jobs to pay for the things they want in life. Then when they get sick, they need to make a choice to get help. If they choose not to, they get sicker. And, Van, I can't let you be around that anymore. It's not healthy or safe. And you know Daddy always wants you safe."

"Yeah." She didn't say anything for long moments and when she did, it rocked the ground under me. "Where's Rylynn? She hasn't come back."

Talking about Rylynn didn't help. Nothing helped. "Rylynn had to leave to go back to Sumner."

"Did she leave because of Greer?"

My back straightened. After the revelations of the day with Sophia, this didn't bode well only adding salt to an already gaping wound. "Why would you say that?"

"Because at the party Greer said you loved Sophia and Rylynn needed to leave so you'd be a family." She paused and bit her bottom lip. "Am I going to be part of your family too?"

"Come here." She came and climbed on my lap. "You are my world. You'll always be my family. Forever." She smiled bright. "Tell me what you heard Greer say."

"Just that you always choose Sophia. She was your true love. But that's not true because you picked my mom." The innocence of a child. I wished she'd stay that way forever. Even knowing the shit that was thrown at her by her mother, she still had that naiveté.

"Right." I kissed the top of her head. "Are you done eating?" She nodded. "Go pick out a movie to watch."

Rylynn had seen the kiss between me and Sophia at the club. Then had Greer's words rolling through her head. That's what she meant about me needing my family. I'd fucked up, my son added to it, and all of it pissed me off. One thing I knew, I needed to get to Rylynn and do it now.

Van hopped down as I pulled out my phone.

"Hello?" Kara asked hesitantly.

"Need you to come over and watch Van for a couple of days."

"What?"

"The only question you have is 'what time'."

She stilled on the line then said, "I'll be there in twenty."

Hated leaving my girl, but Rylynn was coming home. Everything that was broke, I'd damn well fix again.

CHAPTER FOURTEEN
Rylynn

Either Irwin and Snider already had a talk about what happened that night, or they were telling the truth because they were both on the same page. The fact that Snider's dad grounded him for not speaking up sooner and threatened to take away his car and phone if he didn't tell the truth, I was betting on the latter.

Showing up to their doorstep this morning didn't go over so hot at first. It was the father this time who put his foot down for information. The thing that sucked ass was he gave me nothing new to go on.

This meant that Elizabeth either climbed out of the window or someone grabbed her out of it. She sure as shit wasn't going to make it down the fucking toilet.

The police report had the fingerprints found on the windowsill and came up with the mother and father of the property, but nothing else. Not even the kid who lived there had left prints. They stated that the grass wasn't depressed on the ground, but it could've bounced back that night.

The cars at the party were all tagged, the owners, the parents, allowing for fingerprinting. The only one who had her prints was her friend Penny, which was expected since they went together.

The report stated that there were no unusual tracks, which was a bunch of shit because of the number of cars at this party there were a shit ton of tracks. There was no direct path out of the house. Cops just couldn't pick out the unusual because of all the cars.

Every bit of my energy went into finding Elizabeth, keeping all of my focus on it instead of other things.

The damn reports were burned in my brain having gone over them looking for something that was missed. The cops did a great job in finding all the information available. I had to give them that.

It was thorough and detailed. The fact that they came to a dead end didn't surprise me. The more I stared at those reports, the more I willed them to talk to me. Nothing had.

I wasn't giving up. There had to be something in there that would help find this girl.

The police asked her friends if they thought Elizabeth would run away from home, and not one said yes.

She wasn't that type of girl was written so many times in that damn report that it was the only thing that stuck out to me.

The problem was, where would she find the money to disappear. She hadn't used her name because it didn't show up on any searches. The credit card she had from her parents was never touched during her time missing. Her ID also never pinged in the system.

She went up in a puff of smoke that night. Combing through these files was leading me to the same conclusion as the cops. I hated that, but everything made me come up empty.

Elizabeth's parents had called me twice wanting to know if I found anything. Telling them no was difficult but necessary. While I knew they had hope and I did too, any news would've made their healing better. I just couldn't give that to them.

Searching for her friend Penny was becoming a real challenge. Every way to contact her from the police records came up empty. I'd driven by the house dozens of times, always empty. Even left a note on the door and in the mailbox, nothing. She was my key. Finding her would lead to answers. I knew it down to my soul.

Coffee in hand, I stopped dead in front of my house on the sidewalk. A very familiar bike was parked at the curb, the sun shining off the black and red paint job. My breath caught and feet wouldn't move.

Crow was here. At my place. And since I didn't see him around anywhere, he must have already been inside. Fuck, I needed to up my alarm system and get better locks.

I should turn around and leave. That was what I told myself I'd do if this situation happened. Now that it was staring me in the face and the man was in *my* space, entering and confronting him was my only option. Backing down wasn't me, and I wouldn't change for any man. Ever.

He'd never once strayed from my thoughts. Even working my cases, he was there in the back of my mind taunting me. Making me feel when I didn't want to. It wouldn't shut off, no matter what I did. There were times I'd feel his fingertips glide over my skin and goose bumps would rise to the surface, only to turn and it was a mirage.

Then there were the times I would see him kissing Sophia, and the hurt came back full force and the ache in my chest became too much. Closing it off was difficult. Tapping it down and not letting it surface was possible by keeping busy.

Now though, he was waiting for me on the other side of the door.

Turning the handle of the door, it was unlocked as I expected. As I pushed through, Crow was the first thing I saw, sprawled out on the couch, ankles crossed and stretched out in front of him, hands behind his head like he didn't have a care in the world and was meant to be in my space.

It was hot. So damn hot it made my knees weak. Not seeing him for days but thinking of him, the real thing was better than my thoughts. Not only that, I'd seen the heart that beats in his chest, the man he was with his brothers, how he was with his little girl and with me. All of it rushed back and hit me in the gut so hard I had to try to not flinch from the pain of it all. Wanting it, but not being able to have it. Fuck him for being here.

"Well, didn't know there was a party. Did you bring the chips?"

His lip tipped and my heart fluttered, but no chance in hell it would show. He had enough of me, there was no more to give him.

"Forgot. Came to get somethin'."

I tossed my bag to the small table and sat down in the recliner with my coffee, taking a sip. "Sorry didn't know you'd be here or I'd have gotten you one." I held up the coffee.

He said nothing so I asked, "What did you forget?"

"You."

Leaning my head back in the chair my eyes focused on the ceiling. God, I wanted that. Wanted him to come to me and tell me those exact things, grab me and make me whole once again. But it wasn't true. I wasn't the one in his heart. Just a fuck he could play around with.

"Know what Greer told you, and I thought you were smarter than that."

That pissed me right the hell off. He sounded like my damn father. How dare he. How dare he say that shit to me when it was his actions that caused this entire thing in the first place. Fury boiled inside of me as I stared him in the eyes.

"Oh, I'm sorry. You kissing Sophia at your house wasn't bad enough while I was in said house, and we'd just gotten done having sex and you asked me to stay in Rebellion with you. No, that wasn't enough; you had to go and do it again in the middle of the club for everyone to see. Not one of those men blinked at it telling me this wasn't an unusual thing for you. All of it making me the idiot. The whore. Especially when I thought we had something. It was all a load of shit. You should just leave."

"You're not a fuckin' whore. You know that shit," he growled.

My head shook. "I am. Can you just leave?" This time I really believed I was. In the beginning, when it was going to be a one-night stand, I never thought of myself as a whore. This though, now—the way he treated me. I did.

"You saw both times?"

My eyes rolled as the dagger went deep in my

heart. It physically hurt to breathe. He knew he did it. Knew that his lips were on hers. I needed this done with and he needed to leave, refusing to show him any emotion except for anger. That was the only one he got from me now. "It doesn't matter. Life goes on. You need to go." I took a drink of my coffee, the caffeine much needed, but wished it had some bourbon in it for an extra kick. Now was the time I needed the bottle.

"Life doesn't fuckin' go on. Life sucks without you in it."

My world stopped and heart clutched. If only it were that simple. If only those words washed away all the pain inside. If it could only wipe all the memories of thinking Crow was mine, but never really was out it would be perfect. All of it. Life didn't always give us those options though.

My voice was a bit softer than I wanted it to be, but there was no changing it. "I'll never be second to anyone, Crow. Never. Been around a lot of shit, but one thing I always knew in my life was I'd never be the runner-up to any man. I'm not some consolation prize. The next best thing when a man didn't get what he really wanted. A man should want me and only me. Not go off and kiss another woman. If not, if I'm not his number one, the guy isn't worth it. I'm better than that."

"You're right." I was, but I didn't need to hear it from him. It only dug the knife deeper as he continued. "Sophia's the mother of my kid. Loved her for many years. The kiss at the house was all her. She instigated it."

Keeping my mouth shut was hard, but if he wanted the rope to hang himself, who was I to stop him. Sooner he did it, the faster he could get out of my house and my life.

"Should've stopped it. That's on me. I don't remember kissing her at the club. I was drunk; know that's not a fuckin' excuse, but it's the truth."

"Glad we got that ironed out. You can go now." Lifting my cup to my lips, I took a healthy swallow feeling the burn of the heat all the way down and hitting my gut. Bourbon would not be a miss right about now.

"It sure as fuck isn't ironed out, Rylynn. You think I would be here if it was?"

My head shook. "Don't know. Trying to save face to my father or maybe yours. I don't know. But I'm out of this game, Crow. We had good times. The fuckin' best, but I'm not doing this."

"Game, this shit is not a game, Pixie. What I feel for Sophia is not what I feel for you. Hers is a friendship that spans many years and has a child in the mix." He wasn't pleading, he was relaxed and calm. Part of me wanted him to get mad, get angry as hell and start yelling. Like I said before, anger I could work with.

"She loves you and wants to be with you, Crow.

And from the looks of it, you want the same thing. Can't blame you for that," I cut in.

He sighed heavy at that giving me a crack in his cool, calm demeanor. "Yeah, know she does. We've talked. She knows it isn't going to happen. That boat sailed years ago, but she'll always be in my life. We have Greer together, and that'll never change. Can I make you a promise my lips will never come in contact with hers? Yeah, I can because I don't want her in my bed next to me every night. I don't want her riding my cock. That's for you and only you."

A small chuckle left my lips. "This sounds like a horrible romance movie and in the end, I'm the bumbling idiot. Except I'm not. I know who I am. I know what I want. You don't grow up in the Ravage MC and watch everyone around you find their ol' men and ladies seeing how they came to be and not want that for yourself. I deserve that something special too. What I don't want is to watch the man who held my heart in his hands kiss another woman in front of a room filled with his brothers, other charters, loads of women and my family, letting all of them know that I was nothing but a piece of ass."

He started to talk, but I held my hand up.

"Crow, this isn't my first rodeo with the club. You think your brothers don't see me just as that, you're in denial. I welcomed all your guests into your home and stood beside you through everything. They all saw me at your place, like I'd lived there for years welcoming them and chatting it up, offering them food and drinks. All the while, I could've been any one of the club mommas doing that. Hell, I could've been Kara and it wouldn't have mattered. Because once you kissed Sophia in front of everyone, it crushed whatever we started to build. That was the ultimate disrespect, and I'm not some bubbling airhead who lets you have a pass on that."

He leaned forward scooting as close to me as possible without getting up. "You're not a fuckin' idiot, Rylynn. I fucked up, know that and comin' here to own that. Never meant to disrespect you in any way. Fuck, it kills me I did that to you."

I shrugged feeling anything but brushing it off, but trying with everything inside of me to keep my shit together and not crumble to the ground.

"You're mine and only mine. No one else comes close to you, Rylynn. Swore I'd never do this shit. Fall for someone like this. But here I am puttin' it out there. Want you on the back of my bike. Want you livin' in my house. Want to build a family with you. Want you, Rylynn."

Tears welled up in my eyes because I wanted that too. So damn much it killed what was left of me inside because I'd never have it with Crow.

Austyn told me once when she hooked up with

Ryker that they fought like mad, but deep inside she knew he was going to be her future.

When I hooked up with Crow the second time, I'd thought here was my chance. My chance at feeling what Austyn did. A chance to have what she did with someone who cared. Then he kissed another then watched me ride away.

Stupid me, I was the one who got on the back of his bike and went to Rebellion with him thinking there was more there than it was.

It just wasn't the right time for me. And he wasn't the right man.

"I'm not yours, Crow. Thought I would be, but I'm not. It's just not in our cards." I rose from my chair, went into the kitchen, and pulled out the bottle from the top shelf. Fuck it. Twisting the cap off, I removed the lid to my coffee and poured it in needing something stronger to drink.

His heat hit me, then his hands at my hips squeezed. His body forced the gun in the back of my jeans to press into my back. Pulling it out and putting a round in his thigh sounded really good about now. Maybe it would knock some sense into him.

"You are, Pixie. From the first time we were together, you were. Didn't fuckin' realize it until later, but it's true."

He spun me around, but I kept my eyes at his chest

not wanting him to see the pain in mine. He just needed to get back on his bike and ride back to Rebellion. Be with his kids and whoever else he wanted to. That person just wasn't me, and him being here was a pain all on its own.

"Pixie."

My head shook. I didn't want to hear that name anymore. Wanted it erased from his head for the rest of time. Once I loved it. Now, I loathed it because it hurt too bad.

His hand came to my chin and tried to lift it up, but I refused to let it move.

"Please look at me."

My throat clogged and nose started to sting. I couldn't cry. I wouldn't. He didn't get that part of me. The one few people ever got to see. That wasn't his to have. As much as I wanted to let it all flow, it had to be stopped. He wasn't mine.

His scent filled my nostrils, and for once I didn't want to remember the smell. For once I didn't want to suck it in so deep that I'd never forget him. Because it was already there and no matter the time that spanned in my life, it would never leave. Ever.

"Can you please just go?" I asked instead of looking up at him, needing him to leave so I could crumble to the floor.

"Please look at me." This time there was a bit of pleading in his voice, but I didn't respond to it. Couldn't or I'd break.

"I need you to step back and leave, Crow. This is done, and you stayin' in my space when I've asked you to go isn't cool." My hands balled into fists in front of me. Not that I'd hit him, but it was the only thing keeping me in the moment and away from letting everything inside of me come out. I heaved in deep breaths hoping like hell they would calm me and ease the tension building. They didn't.

"Can't leave without you, Pixie. Need you."

That was all I could take. I was done. I'd always been a strong person, my mom and dad instilled that. But this was different. This was a trial of the heart. One that I'd just ran through with my grandpa, but even death had a difference in the pain.

This one was alive and beating, standing in front of me wanting more from me.

"You broke it, Crow. It can't be fixed."

"That's not true," he said immediately. That was when the tear slid down my cheek unable to hold it back anymore. He was going to get more of me, and here I thought I had nothing else to give. But he was going to get my pain because that was what he did to me. Sliced me open to bleed all over.

I gave it to him by lifting my face to his and connecting with his eyes, letting him see the devastation there. Then the words came spewing out. "You held my heart in your hands. Was scared shitless, but I believed in you. Believed in us. What we were building was something I wanted to explore, but that can't happen now, Crow, and you need to be man enough to accept that and leave."

"I'm man enough for a lot of shit, Pixie, but givin' you up isn't something either of us wants." His fingers brushed the silent tears away from my eyes. It was a sweet gesture that only added to the agony of the situation.

"Please leave, Crow."

"You're mine, Pixie. Only mine."

That was when I lost my shit. It didn't happen often in my life, twice if I remembered correctly, but my father's temper was engrained in me. I was able to keep it in check most of the time, using a smartass comment to lessen whatever was going on at the time. But there were times when the rage took over. When I wasn't the person anyone thought I was. When the anger beat into me so hard anything was possible.

My face cleared as my eyes glared and hands went to his chest. "Get out of my fucking house," I spoke low and meaningful.

His eyes flashed. "Not gonna happen unless you're on the back of my bike."

The laugh was menacing as my father's, and my blood grew red hot. "Never. Get out." That was when I moved fast, getting out from under him and pulling the gun from my jeans. "Mean it, Crow. Get out."

"You're gonna shoot me?"

I fired one at his feet letting him know I meant business. Fuck him. He didn't even jump at it. Instead, he came at me like a bull. I wanted to pull the trigger. I wanted to end whatever this was. I wanted him to just stop.

But I couldn't do it. I couldn't put a bullet in him.

He knocked the gun out of my hand. All of my moves not working on him. It seemed he knew them all before I even started. He had me subdued, and the red-hot anger melted away. It was one thing that I hated about it when it came to the fact that it went away too damn fast.

Tears fell from my eyes freely as Crow turned me around in his arms. "Know you're hurtin', Pixie. Know I caused your pain, and never in my life meant to do that shit. But I'm not givin' up. You're too important to me to ever give you up."

"Then why did you do it?"

"Because I'm an asshole who's never had an ol' lady before and didn't think about my actions."

My head fell into his chest as his arms went around me tight, holding me to him. He scooped me up, and we were moving. He sat on the couch putting me on his lap. I burrowed my head in his chest trying to pull my shit together but coming up short.

"Pixie, I'm so fuckin' sorry." He rocked me back and forth. My tears were silent, and my body was still as I allowed myself to have a brief moment to pull my head out of my ass.

It felt so damn nice being in his arms again. I hated myself for even thinking it. As he rubbed my back and kissed the top of my head it only got better. Dammit.

After a long time of being like this, I was able to breathe again, but he didn't stop holding me. "Need time, Crow."

"Time's too precious to waste," he retorted.

He was right, but where my heart was concerned it had to be taken. Therefore, I said nothing.

He let out a long breath. "You're mine, Rylynn. Even if you're not on the back of my bike or in my bed, you're mine. Everyone is gonna know it. I can't let you go. I won't let you go. We'll get past this."

"How do I get past you loving another woman, Crow?"

"I don't. Haven't loved her that way in a long damn time. Fucked up, baby. Know it and own it."

My heart continued to throb. "Do you realize how much I want to believe you? How much I want to just let it all go and forget it ever happened? I can't. That trust that I was building with you was damaged in a way that I don't think it can be rebuilt."

"It can and it will."

He sounded so sure of himself, and I didn't know what to think. Everything was swirling around me jumbled up in my head. Love made people do stupid shit all the time. I just never thought it would be in my lap to find.

"Need time." I made a move to get up from his lap, but he held me tight. "Please let me go, Crow. Need time, and you need to give it to me. Know it's hard for you to do, but I'm asking you to give me time."

His arms lessened just enough for me to get up.

"Need you to go so I can have that time, Crow."

It was then I took a chance and saw it in his eyes, face, and demeanor. He was hurting. I hated that for him, I really did. But he needed to give me this. This situation was on him and if he didn't give it to me, we'd be over in every way possible. "Please," I said one more time as he got up from the couch to stand in front of me.

Grasping me and pulling me into him, he kissed me hard, wet, and deep as my knees went weak and tears flowed with purpose.

He pulled away then swiped the tears from my face. "I'll be back," he said, giving me one more kiss on the lips, then he was gone.

I fell to the couch, curled into a ball, and allowed everything inside of me to flow.

I was broken. Shattered. Devastated.

A mess.

He was both my pain and my peace.

CHAPTER FIFTEEN
Crow

PISSED DIDN'T EVEN CUT THROUGH WHAT I FELT RIGHT now as I pulled into the Sumner Ravage MC parking lot and parked my bike. There were quite a few in the lot, but I had one man in my mind to see.

"Crow!" Austyn yelled, coming up to me and wrapping her arms around my neck. She needed this and I gave it to her, trying to push what I was feeling out, but not being able too.

"Hey," I said as she pulled away.

"I'm so excited you're here! Dad didn't say anything about it."

That's when the gravelly voice came from my left. "That's because I didn't know." Cruz came up, shook my hand, and gave me a one-handed hug. "What's goin' on?" he asked me, eyeing me up and down.

That was when the air around us changed. We were outside, but that didn't matter. It felt as if we were in a small room with the oxygen constricting.

I knew exactly who it came from.

I'd wanted it.

It was the reason I was here.

Not to see Cruz, my brothers, or sister.

No. I came because I needed to see him face to face.

From the fire breathing out of Rhys, he knew I fucked up with his daughter huge. He knew what I'd done and had every right to be pissed at me. Christ help whoever treated my girl like that.

I deserved it.

Craved it.

Needed it.

Needed the punishment.

Cruz stepped in front of me as Rhys marched directly for me. "Cruz. Move," I ordered, but he didn't. "Now," I barked a bit louder.

Since Cruz didn't move I did meeting Rhys just in time for him to swing and connect with my jaw. Blood spewed from my lip, spraying to the blacktop as I turned back to him and charged him, catching him in the ribs.

He grunted, swung again, and clocked me in the shoulder, then I got him in the throat. It took him a few minutes to recover from that one as it knocked the wind out of him.

"Fucker," he grumbled, coming back at me full force. Cruz stepped in front of him, and I darted to the side where Rhys' lurched at me.

Punch after punch was thrown.

Blood ran down my face, but neither of us backed down. Just kept going after one another over and over again.

"Fuckin' love her, man." I told Rhys something I hadn't even told Rylynn yet, but it was true. She was it for me. She was my end game. Didn't fucking deserve her one bit, but loved her all the same.

He swung connecting with my ribs and jabbing twice, and I jolted. "Great way of showin' it. All over another piece at your clubhouse. Asshole. She deserves more."

That was when I really knew how close Rylynn was with her father. She'd told him everything. It was my cross to bear. I blocked, then he hit me in the eye. "Fucked up."

He went for the face again, but I ducked getting him in the abs. "Ya think, motherfucker?" he got out without missing a beat, landing a hard one to my ribs.

Rhys was a beast and going to take every hit I gave him. While I was in the wrong, I was also Ravage and not a pussy. Rhys would really have no respect for me if I gave him nothing back. As much as he needed to hurt me, I needed it in return.

A motorcycle roared in the distance, but I didn't

pay any mind to it. That sound was everywhere and became a knowing sound everywhere I went.

I landed a blow to his eye, and he returned the favor again. Arms wrapped around my middle pulling me back as I fought to keep upright. I needed Rhys to kick my ass. Needed to feel his anger for what I did. Needed him to take it out on me and put me through the wringer.

I relished the fucking pain.

It was better than feeling like a dickhead to Rylynn.

Arms wrapped around Rhys as he started back for me.

"Enough," Cruz barked hard and rough, gaining everyone's attention.

"What in the hell is goin' on here!" Rylynn screamed, coming to stand next to Cruz, between her father and me, but her eyes were my way. "You came to beat up my dad?"

"Fuck if he beat me up," Rhys grumbled, still pissed as hell and fighting the grip on him. There were two guys on him though. I still thought if he really wanted to, he could break away and come at me again. Same with me. If I really wanted to, I could get away as well, but seeing Rylynn stopped me from breaking free.

Two men loving the same woman in two totally different ways. Life threw some fucked up shit. As a father, I felt his anger. As a man, I felt it just the same. Fuck, I hated this shit.

Rylynn got up in my face, standing on her tiptoes to get at eye level. She was tall, but not as much as me. "I told you I needed space." She flung out her hands as the ones holding me let go. "And this is how you do that? By coming here and hitting my father?"

I wouldn't lie to her, so I said nothing. Rhys needed to beat the shit out of me. I deserved it. We both knew it. He knew the score. I knew the score. Never back down. Ever.

Rhys was coming up hard and fast behind Rylynn. I grabbed her quick and pressed her against my back. It was so fast she didn't have time to complain or bitch. It also made Rhys come up short. I was prepared for him. Ready to take what he was going to give me and make for damn sure nothing touched Rylynn.

He scanned me from top to toe. It took him a few beats and as Rylynn tried to come out from behind my back, I grabbed her again holding her with one arm. The other at the ready for whatever was about to happen. Because it wasn't going to be pretty.

"You fucked up," Rhys said instead of swinging.

"Yep. Already said that."

Rylynn yelled, "Stop boxing me in!" as she tried to swing back around to get away. Luckily, I kept her where she needed to be, even if she was punching my back. Not that I thought her father would hurt her. It was just instinct to protect her in any way that I could.

Rhys pointed behind me. "That one. You have to earn."

"Damn right, and I'm fuckin' doin' it."

"We'll see." He turned on his boot and stormed into the clubhouse. Only then did I let Rylynn go and when I did, she was breathing fury. Every bit of it I was ready to take.

"I can't believe you just fought my dad!" she barked up at me, hands on her hips and attitude up to a thousand percent. Damn, she was beautiful.

Her eyes looked all over me, but she didn't need to feel anything for the bloodshed. It may not have needed to happen like this, but it needed to be done. He was pissed and needed to let it out. Me, I was just pissed and needed a good fight. Win-win.

"Pixie."

"Don't you Pixie me! I can't believe you right now. I tell you I need time and you come here and fight." She looked at my face. Her eyes hit mine. Connected. She softened only slightly, but I would take whatever I could get. "Come on. Let's get you cleaned up." She grabbed my hand, but I pulled her to me instead and kissed her hard and fast.

She pulled back with my blood on her. "Seriously?" she said, letting go of my hand and marching into the clubhouse. I followed behind feeling the blood running down my face.

Cruz came up to me and slapped me on the shoulder. "Well that was a good way to welcome you into the family." He chuckled, and my lip tipped.

"Yeah. It's somethin' alright."

THE PARTY WAS in full swing. Even telling the Sumner Ravage that I didn't need it, they still put it together on the fly. One thing these people knew how to do was throw a bash.

After getting cleaned up and having Rylynn ream my ass a few more times, people started showing up. People who included some of my family it seemed.

I'd met Pops before, several times, but had to say this time was different.

"Son," he said, coming up to me, holding his hand out, and giving me a one-handed hug. Fuck, I had a grandpa. Strange.

"Hey." I returned the gesture as he released me and stood back.

"Sorry about not makin' it to your father's service. The doc's been keepin' an eye on me and had to go in for tests. He was a great man, Crow."

"Yes, he was. Thanks for that."

"Know this is all kinds of fucked up, but we'll

manage." His ol' lady, Ma, came up to us. "You remember Ma?"

She didn't hesitate to wrap me in her arms tight and hold me for a while. Her body shook. Fuck, another woman crying on me today. "It's alright," I tried to comfort as she pulled back.

"You're so big. I just." She shook her head. "Sorry."

"It's a weird situation. We're all gaining our legs."

"So sorry about your dad, Crow. He was a good man." Damn. My grandma, who just found out she was, still gave the respect to my father that was deserved. These people. They were... Great.

"I am too."

She smiled wide. "Now I hear that I have some great-grandbabies who need to be spoiled. We need to set up a time for us to come out there and get to know your kids."

"Ma, the man just found out he has us, don't throw us in his face," Pops said, and it made me smile. "Let the man get to know us then we can meet the kids." He looked at me. "She's a little excited about the prospect of having great-grandkids."

"Understandable."

I felt someone staring at me, looked and saw Rylynn. Giving her a soft smile, she returned it but turned away quickly. Fuck, that was going to be an uphill battle.

The second introduction came from a ten-year-old

little girl who I knew immediately was Rylynn's baby sister because they looked just like each other.

"Hi, I'm Mazie," she said, holding out her hand.

I knelt down and took it, giving it a shake. "I'm Crow."

Two seconds I was kneeling, the next I was flat on my ass as Mazie pushed me down then stood over top of me. "That's for hitting my daddy!" she said, storming away.

Bursting out laughing, the sun was blocked and looking up it was my girl. She held out her hand to me. I clasped it and went with her as she *pulled* me up. "She's a little protective."

"Ya think?"

Rylynn was smiling, something I'd much rather see her do than cry. I wrapped her in my arms as she looked up at me. When she closed her eyes and tried to take a step back, I kissed her. In front of all her family, the club, her father—everyone. I didn't give a fuck. She was mine and would always be mine. She needed to know it. They needed to know it.

Only after I was done, did I let her go. She moved away from me, her hand to her lips going into the clubhouse.

"You know..." Austyn started as I turned to her, her face alight. "Rylynn's a tough woman."

A chuckle escaped me. "Know that one."

"No, you really don't."

She took me over to a picnic table to the opposite side where few people were conversing. We sat on the top of it, our feet resting on the actual seat. Me and my sister. Fuck, that was strange. Growing up an only child, never thought this was something I'd have and wasn't quite sure how I felt about it.

"Then tell me."

"And what fun would that be? I want to see her kick your ass."

I chuckled. "That would be funny you say?"

"My mom and Riley taught her a lot. You'd be surprised."

"She's already put a woman on her ass at my house. Not that the bitch didn't deserve it, but I know she's tough."

She leaned her elbows to her knees. "Not just that though. It's her." She shrugged. "You jacked shit up, but you know it. People talk around here. You show her you're not that man. And let me tell you, you do that, you'll be the richest man in Alabama. Because she's everything, Crow. Total package."

Looking over at her smiling face, I said, "You're right." Wrapping my arm around her, I pulled her into my body giving her a side hug. She melted into me.

"I want to get to know you, Crow. And your kids. Please don't shut us out."

A large huff of breath escaped. "Gonna do my best. Everything'll work out in the end."

"Let's hope."

Nothing like a heart to heart with the sister you never knew you had.

It was after the food was consumed and everyone was settling in when Cooper approached. I was sitting by the fire outside when he sat next to me.

Rylynn had been giving me a wide berth that I was tired of and planned on making it very narrow very soon. There was no hiding. She needed time. She had until the party was over. That was as much as she was going to get.

"Isn't this the end all be all," Cooper said next to me, taking a drink of his beer. As I looked out among the Sumner Ravage MC, everyone welcomed me with open arms. Everyone but Rhys and Mazie, that was.

Even knowing them through the brotherhood, knowing them as true family was something to get used to. Especially now that my dad was in the ground. It made it all even more strange.

"You're tellin' me."

"So we gonna see you around here more?" he asked straight out.

"Visits, but bein' straight with ya. Here for Rylynn. This was just a bonus." Grabbing my beer off the table, I took a swallow.

"Get that one." He chuckled. "Funny, once you get a taste, you just fuckin' know."

"Is this brother to brother advice here?"

He grinned wider. "Somethin' like that." The grin faded. "There's nothin' we can do about the past. Can't change it or rearrange it. Know your dad was a good man. Never want to shit on his memory either. The thing is our dad is a good man too. Know it'll be jacked up. Know it won't be easy, but get to know him not just as the president of the club, but as father and son."

"Does this mean that we have thirty plus years of fightin' to make up for?"

He laughed full out again. "Nah. That's where we got lucky. Don't have to go through that bullshit to see the other side." His hand came to my shoulder. "Family can never be too big. Know you have one in Alabama, but you have blood here in Sumner. Don't forget that."

With another squeeze, he was gone. The weight of the past few hours hit me hard. Every step of it was momentous in some way or the other. It was all heavy even though each of them tried to make it light.

During the ride here, all I could think about was getting to Rylynn. All of this—

the party, getting to know people who share the same blood—was a bounty I didn't feel like I deserved. The entire thing was strange, and trying to process it all was hard.

It didn't make my need for Rylynn one bit less. I went in search of Rylynn. Almost to the door, I was stopped with a tight grip on my arm. Turning, Princess stood there. My stepmother. Lord, the bitch was hard as hell, and now she was ...

"Come talk to me," she said, turning around and walking through two doors. Inside was a large ring, but other than that the place was empty. Quiet.

"Need to get your pulse with the family," she said, straight out not beating around the bush. That was what I liked about her. No bullshit. Straight out. Reminded me of Rylynn.

Legs wide, hands in the back pocket of my jeans I answered, "Still alive."

She chuckled. "You are that." She moved around to a set of chairs, nodding her head to one while she sat in the other. Pulling it back a touch I sat. "Cruz, Cooper, Nox, Austyn all of them want to know more about you. My girl is takin' this shit really hard because of the lost time. Need to know that they put their hands out there, you're not gonna chop them off."

I shook my head. "You haven't changed a bit."

"Nope."

"Not choppin' anything off. I want to get to know them too, but straight out, this trip was for Rylynn. She will be on the back of my bike and in Alabama with me. Gettin' all of this was the icing on the cake. 'Preciate it."

"You're not just a brother, you're blood. Now that you have us though, we're like an STD—we never go away."

I burst out laughing. "Did Pixie get her smart mouth from you?"

"Pixie? You call Rylynn Pixie?"

On a shrug, I replied, "Suits her don't ya think? I mean she's sweet as sugar, short with Tinkerbelle hair. It fits."

"So wrong that it does." She paused. "Heard what you did."

"Figured." Too damn bad I left my beer outside on the table. I could use it. One thing I knew was anything and everything was talked about with these people.

"Gonna lay this straight. You fucked up, bad." She told me something I already knew. "You want her as your ol' lady, you fix that shit tonight. You tell her how you feel. Lay it all out for her, Crow. Not shittin' you. Rylynn's grown up here, seen and been involved with her fair share of club life. She's no pushover and can hack anything you throw at her."

"Is this your motherly advice." I tried to joke, but she didn't see it that way.

"No, this is an ol' lady tellin' you if you want the woman, you lay that shit out and fast. Make her see what you do. You fix what you broke immediately."

"That was the plan tonight." I smiled. "Glad to know I was thinkin' the right thing."

"Yeah," she said on a cough. "But know this—you fuck her over, you'll have me to deal with. She's my girl and son or not, you fuck that up again—I'm comin' for ya."

On that, she got up and sauntered out of the room.

In like a tornado, out like a hurricane. That was Princess.

CHAPTER SIXTEEN
Rylynn

LAUGHING, I WAS TRYING TO GET WHAT THE GUY IN front of me was saying. He was in his twenties and just started hanging around the club. This was what men did in Ravage who were interested in prospecting. Therefore, I wasn't sure what this guy knew about the club.

Pouring drinks at the party was his gig and since I needed space from Crow's eyes, I came in here and sat my ass on a bar stool. No way I was loading up on booze though. I needed to be level-headed when it came to Crow.

"So, Rylynn, you come around here much?" It was very sad, but I completely forgot his name and couldn't pull up even the first letter of it. He'd told me right out of the gate, but it wasn't on the tip of my brain.

At the question, it confirmed to me that this guy

didn't know much about the Ravage MC and really should do his homework if he wanted to stick around. Knowing the members and their families was a must. "Yeah, you could say that."

"Maybe I..."

The guy's eyes widened behind me. It could be anyone, especially my father who'd been keeping a tight watch on me, but I knew it wasn't. I could feel him. That special tingle that only he gave me. How was that even possible to feel someone before you saw them? To just know they were there?

"Stay the fuck away from my girl."

The newbie wasn't going to make it. I knew this because I was pretty sure he pissed his pants at Crow's tone. No one got through who didn't have balls. He obviously didn't if just someone's voice made him show fear, and it made me wonder why he was even here. Why be part of a motorcycle club when you couldn't hold your own?

The guy behind me had balls though, big ones. I wanted to be pissed at him for going at it with my father, but knowing my dad and how protective he was in all aspects of my life, Crow wouldn't have just stood there and let my dad pound him into the ground.

There was little doubt that Crow gave as good as he got, but still, it didn't mean I had to like it.

"Sorry, man. I didn't..." The hang around started.

"No, you fuckin' didn't. Get gone," Crow interrupted, his hands coming to my shoulders behind me and giving me a squeeze. I didn't want to love his touch, but fuck me I did. Damn him.

The hang around did as told, moving quickly into the kitchen and out of sight.

"Pretty sure he pissed himself," I said to the bar as Crow leaned down in my ear.

"Need to get out of here, Pixie." I turned around and looked up at him. Damn, he was gorgeous. The man I could love for the rest of my life and never look at another. The man who had a heart larger than he let anyone know. The way he was with his children, at least, Van. His determination, strength, and presence. All of it making him the man who stood behind me.

Damn him.

"No one's stoppin' ya."

His head dipped low into mine. "You're comin' with me."

"I am huh?" My arms crossed over my chest. Fuck, I wanted to, really bad, but I didn't trust it. Didn't trust him. Even after watching him with his brothers and sister, I just didn't know if I could put myself out there again. He'd hurt me and there was a possibility of him doing it again. Only it would be worse. I couldn't go through that again. It would completely destroy me.

"Yes."

"Are you high?" I challenged.

His brow quirked. He didn't answer because his

mouth was on mine. The music, people, everything disappeared, and it was just me and Crow in the middle of the bar. It was beauty. And I hated myself for craving it so badly, but also didn't tear myself away from him. I'd missed his lips, his touch, him. Love was a mean sonuvabitch.

A loud bang happened beside us on the bar as I jumped, breaking from Crow and turning to it. Nox stood there smiling.

"Get a room," Nox said, hitting Crow's shoulder. "While we'd love to see this shit play out, unless you want another go around with her father ..." He trailed off and nodded toward my dad, who had a scowl on his face. Shit.

"Don't give a fuck about that," Crow said, bending down and attaching his lips to mine. He picked me up, and my legs had no choice but to go around his hips.

I melted. My body disconnected from my brain, and I gave in. Somehow, some way, we made it outside with catcalls everywhere. We didn't stop until we were at his bike, and he put my feet to the ground.

As we looked into each other's eyes my heart began to thump overtime. Indecision hit me creating a war between mind and body. What I wanted and what I should do were on different pages threatening to tear me in two pieces.

"I'm stayin' with you," he said boldly. "On my bike."

It was true. I was going to hell because without

another thought at his words, I was on the back of his bike and we were through the gates of the clubhouse and going down the road. Once again, I had nothing on me. This time not even my phone. It was probably still sitting at the bar.

The ride to my house wasn't long, but I enjoyed hanging on to Crow the entire way. I'd ridden my bike to the club earlier and it was nothing compared to riding behind Crow.

He parked and we both swung off in front of my place. "Guess I'm the Holiday Inn tonight."

Crow pulled me into his body, bringing me super close. "No. You're Rylynn. The woman I want next to me for the rest of my fucking life."

My heart skittered and breaths caught, but before I could say anything, his lips were on mine. When we made it up to the door, and I was able to break away in order to get it unlocked and opened. He came at me in my apartment, but I held my hand out. As much as it killed, we had shit to talk about.

"Want a beer or bourbon?" I asked, moving into the kitchen and grabbing the bottle from the top cabinet, setting it down on the countertop knowing it was stupid, but needing something because his closeness was making me want things I couldn't have.

"Neither," he said in the doorway of the kitchen and held out his hand. Closing my eyes and taking a deep breath, I took it.

He led me to the couch, this time him sitting on one end and me on the other. Guess he knew we needed to talk as well.

Blowing out a deep breath, I pulled my legs up and tucked them my ass. "You kissed another woman. That's a no-go for me, Crow. If it's me, it's only me. End of discussion," I started. "Do you understand how much that hurt seeing your lips on someone else. Feeling the pain of that sear through you? I'll never do that again, Crow. Ever."

"If it were you who had your lips on another man, I'd kill him. No doubt about it in my mind. So I get it. What you need to understand is from this moment on, you are all I want and need. There is no other. There is nothing if you're not in my life. You're my light in the darkness. Without you, I'm just dark."

"No, you're not..." I started, but he interrupted me.

"Yeah, Pixie. I am. I know it and chose it. But you are my light. The one. You're mine."

The damn tears welled up in my eyes, and I had to breathe in and out to get them to stop. No tears!

"Come back to Rebellion so I can prove it to you. Swear you won't regret it."

How could a heart break and mend in such a small amount of time? That I didn't think I'd ever have the answer to. But I loved him. Love made us do stupid shit, like giving the man who shredded you another shot.

If it was meant to be, I needed to find out, and we couldn't do that with me a state away.

"*If* I do, I will never be okay with any woman putting their lips on you or touching you in that *come and fuck me* way that you know women do. It happens, Crow, they're dead and I'm gone. And I don't just mean gone from your life, I mean gone as in you won't find me again."

Being a PI, many resources were at my disposal. Finding a new identity wouldn't be hard. But he and I both knew staying away from my family was a no go. I would though disappear for him.

He gripped my hands. "I'll shut it down immediately."

I wanted to believe him with everything inside of me. How did you trust someone who broke your heart? How did you move on from all the heartbreak to start over again? Guess I was about to find out.

"Never again, Crow. You're either all in with this, or it's not going to work."

He pulled me into his lap holding me close. "I'm all in, baby. Love you. Want to be with you and only you. You won't have to wonder because I'll fuckin' prove it every damn day."

Breathing in and out. My mind swirled. There were two options here. One: make him leave, tear my heart in two, and never know if we worked. Or two: give this a try and risk my heart being broken.

Either way, my heart was going to break. I would regret it if we didn't try. Never knowing if what we went through led us to being sealed in strength or to end in disaster.

"Trust is a huge thing for me, Crow, and I don't know if I can get it back between us." My voice was soft, almost silent. My mom and dad taught me a lot. The biggest thing over everything else was trust and loyalty. Crow broke that.

"We will. I'll bust my balls to show you." He kissed my lips briefly. "Trust is hard for a man like me, but I've let you in more than anyone else in my life. I'll get yours back. You'll see the kind of man I am."

"I want to believe you."

His hands moved up and down my arms causing a shiver. "And I want to be believed."

I looked down feeling the wetness threaten to take over. Being vulnerable wasn't my thing, and being it in that moment was a tough pill to swallow. I was. Incredibly so.

His fingertips came to my chin, and he raised it so our eyes met. Different emotions tumbled through his. "Rylynn." He started my name with a gentle caress. "I'm in love with you."

Tears welled up as he continued, "I keep thinking back to that night in the clubhouse." My chest compressed, and I made a move to get up. "Wait." He held me in place.

"I don't think I want to hear this," I told him honestly.

"Yes, you do." He kissed my lips once again, and I shut up. "At the clubhouse, I never saw Sophia." At the name, my stomach turned. "Baby. I never did. Every memory I have of that night, you were it. I don't know why or the how, and I'm so damn sorry."

"So every time you get drunk at the clubhouse, I'm going to have to worry that you're cheating on me?" That was a pain all its own. Trust. Gone.

"No. There are no excuses for what I did. I'm sorry. Down to my fucking soul sorry." Wetness pooled in his eyes and my heart broke for him. "We can fix this."

"How?" I asked as the tears rolled down my face. "It's too much."

"It's only too much if we let it be."

My head shook. "Love doesn't always fix the problems. As much as we want it to it only has so much power."

His lips touched mine. "You know my cut means the world to me."

I nodded, looking into his eyes.

"Never wanted something more than my cut." He kept on going as I listened attentively. "Until you."

The world stopped. Time stopped. Everything stopped. He wanted me more than his cut? There was no way that was possible. No man would claim that.

With my body frozen, I couldn't move. His words

rolled around in my head over and over again. *Never wanted something more than my cut. Until you.* Holy shit.

Mouth hanging open, I stared at him unable to form words as to how I was feeling. He didn't fill the quiet with words, instead giving them time to sink in.

After a long time, I said, "You can't mean that."

"Wouldn't have said it if I didn't. No man would. It's how much I care and love you. Need you to know the depths of it and fuck." He pulled back, resting his head on the back of the couch. "Never thought I'd ever say those fuckin' words."

"You have to know I'd never ask you to give up the club or your cut. Ever."

He lifted up, and a smirk played at his lip. "You think I don't know that? It's another one of the reasons I love you."

"Don't you think we need time apart to see what we feel?" I asked, my hands on his chest.

"No. You and I both know our time is limited on this earth. Don't want to waste any more of it."

I leaned in and pressed my forehead to his. "I was scared before, Crow. Now, I'm terrified." Raw emotion whipped through me like a cold wind through a cornfield.

"I deserve that, Pixie, and I'll work my ass off to prove to you that the trust we'll build is stronger than granite."

Exhaustion took me over. The tears and feelings becoming too much for the day. "I need sleep, Crow."

He lifted me with ease and led me to the bedroom, setting me gently on the bed. The fire in his eyes told me what he wanted, but I was too raw for it. "Just hold me."

Crow nodded, stripped his clothes while I did mine, and he held me the entire night.

Connected in our pain.

Fueled by the fire between us.

What more could I want for? If only I could believe it was real.

CHAPTER SEVENTEEN
Crow

THE PHONE WOKE ME FROM A PEACEFUL SLEEP. RYLYNN was still in my arms exactly as I'd fallen asleep hours ago. She hadn't moved an inch. Her beautiful hair spread out on my shoulder and the pillow. Her hand on my abs searing heat into me.

I wasn't fucking around last night. Meant every word I said. Surprised the shit out of me. My cut meant everything to me and as soon as those words left my lips, it shocked me to my core. Because they were true. That was how much I loved her. How much I felt for her. How much I wanted her beside me through the good times and the bad. All of it.

Hopefully she felt how much because I needed her to trust me. Needed her to be by my side.

Never had I needed or wanted a woman the way I did her. Ever.

I kissed her temple and reached over to the night-stand grabbing my phone.

The display said *Cruz calling.* I took the call.

"Crow."

"Come over for brunch." Short and to the point Cruz definitely was. Always had been. The fact he's my father didn't change him a bit. Not that I expected it to. What I didn't expect was a phone call this early in the damn morning.

Rylynn shifted, her eyes coming up to mine. I winked, and she blushed. Fuck, that was hot. She hadn't done that before, and I liked it. "What time?"

"Eleven," Cruz said in the phone.

"Right. Later."

He disconnected.

"Who was that?" Rylynn asked in her sleepy, sexy as hell voice.

"Cruz. Wants us over for brunch at eleven."

Rylynn looked over at the clock that read nine thirty-seven. "You should go, and I'll stay here."

I pulled her up my body knowing she hated morning breath, but not giving that first fuck because I kissed her. She tried to push back, but didn't get anywhere. She finally gave in and that was when I pulled away. "You're comin' with me."

Her head fell to the bed in exasperation. "We need time, Crow."

Giving her my weight, I rolled on top of her. "No more time. You're mine. I'm yours. Everything else will work itself out."

"You sound so sure of yourself."

"Because I am." I kissed her once again. "Now, gotta shower and dress. You wanna join me, I'm up for that. Or I can fuck you when we get back."

Her eyes dilated telling me she liked the idea. Her words though were of the contrary. "I'm showering by myself." The little vixen was going to hold out on me. That was fine. I'd wait. Today. Then all bets were off.

"I've never been here before," I told Rylynn as we got off my bike and took our helmets off. Coming to Sumner every now and then, we'd always meet at the clubhouse. This felt different, and I was damn happy to have Rylynn at my back.

She hadn't said a thing this morning about coming to Rebellion with me. I'd let it lay, giving her that time she kept saying she needed. The outcome would be the same no matter what way the coin flipped.

"It's like any other place, Crow. The big difference is you know these people are blood. That's it. Don't think too much on it. Just enjoy it."

I pulled her into me and kissed her hard. "When'd you get so smart?"

"I'm a descendant of Einstein."

Laughter broke through, and it was exactly what I needed to lighten the mood. Somehow this felt so damn serious, and in actuality, it wasn't. It was us eating food.

"Have I told you today that I love you." Her breath caught, eyes wide. "Yeah, Pixie. You'll be hearing those words from me a lot, but my actions will show you. Swear it." Grabbing her hand tight, I pulled her into me and kissed her.

"Would you stop necking and get in here?" Nox yelled from the entryway of the house. Rylynn and I burst out laughing.

"Nothing like getting caught by dad!" Rylynn hollered back at Nox who joined us laughing.

"Aren't you cute, Ry," he teased.

"Damn right. Like a little bunny," she retorted. The back and forth they had was interesting to see. It was as if they were alone in it, and I wasn't sure how I felt about that.

"Bunny my ass. More like a panther coming to rip our throats out."

We walked up to the door. "Damn straight." She tapped Nox on the nose. "And don't you forget it." She walked past him, trying to let go of my hand, but I didn't allow it.

"Awe, she already have you trained?" Nox joked, but my head swung to him. He held up his hands. "Down there, man. Gotta take the teasing if you wanna be in Rylynn's life. She's big on that shit."

Rylynn started hugging people, and we released. "Know that, Nox."

Nox slapped me on the shoulder giving it a good squeeze. "She's not givin' in, is she?"

The question caught me off guard. It was something that people who were really close would recognize. How close were these two? "How'd you know that?"

He shrugged. "She's Rylynn. You fucked up, and you have to pay for that. Once you get done with your penance, it'll be all good."

My arms crossed over my chest. "How is it that you know all of this?"

Nox smiled knowingly. "Grew up together, man."

"Yeah, and…" I prompted him.

He chuckled. "Got nothin' to worry about, Crow. I'm not after your woman. She and I are tight. Just gotta ride her wave for a bit."

Tight. There were so many questions I wanted to ask. The thought of him *going after my woman* pissed me off. Hitting your estranged brother in your estranged family's house wouldn't be good.

"Hey!" Cruz came in doing the one-armed hug thing. His pats on the back were rough, and as we pulled away a huge smile was across his face. "Glad you came."

"I had a choice?" I questioned with a tip of my lip.

"Nope," he answered directly, and I full out smiled. Yeah. This would be okay.

"Sit!" Princess called out, holding a very large platter and setting it on the table, Ma close at her heels.

I held back, Rylynn coming up to me and giving me a soft smile. Why I hung back didn't register. But as everyone sat down it hit me. They each had their place in this family. They knew what it was, and there was zero doubt in it. They'd probably had hundreds of meals around this table, and this was my first.

Two open seats sat next to Cruz with Pops and Ma having moved down. It was intentional, there was no mistaking it.

Fuck me, this felt so surreal.

"Have a seat," Cruz ordered, but it took Rylynn pulling my hand to get my attention. With that action, I sat and looked around the table. Cruz and Princess. Cooper and Bristyl. Austyn and Ryker. Nox and Carsyn. Pops and Ma. If GT's crew were here, it would be all of them.

Food was passed around the table.

"Why didn't we just have it up on the island so we didn't have to do this pass around game," Austyn groaned, telling me that this wasn't normal. It made me feel a little better.

"It's a special day," Ma said diplomatically.

"Welcome to the family, Crow," Austyn said sarcastically. "We don't eat like this... like ever."

"Good. I sure as shit don't." My comment caused laughter, and I felt a bit of the tension drain away. Rylynn reached under the table and grabbed my hand giving it a squeeze, that took even more out.

Damn, I loved her.

Lifting her hand to my mouth, I kissed it. She jolted in shock and looked around the table. For what, I had no clue.

"So does this mean you're moving?" Austyn asked Rylynn.

I felt Rylynn's body tense. Therefore, I answered for her. "Yep."

Austyn's gaze turned to me just as Rylynn's glare hit me full bore. "I haven't decided yet," Rylynn grumbled.

"Uh. Oh. Destruction in paradise," Nox joked.

"We're not talking about this," I said, and Nox's face turned. He didn't mean any harm, but if Rylynn was going to try to shut me down, this day would end very differently. It needed to be calm. Or as calm as I could make it.

"Alright. So touchy subject. Got it," Bristyl commented. "Cooper and I had sex before we came."

"Seriously?" Austyn responded. "I do not need to hear that shit."

"Got you to get off Crow's ass," Bristyl fired back.

"Touché." Austyn went back to her food.

"So," Ma started. "Tell me about my great-grandbabies." She really had a thing for my kids.

"Seriously?" Pops said, setting down his fork. "You just can't let it go, can you?"

Ma slapped Pops' arm. "No. Leave me be."

Pops looked at me. "Sorry, son. She's gonna be at your throat until she knows all about them."

"No problem." I chewed and then swallowed. "I have two. Greer is sixteen. Football player and does pretty good in school."

"Bet you have to cover him with a rubber," Nox said loudly.

At that, I chuckled. "Pretty much. Has this new tutor. One look at the girl and he was told he could only study with her at the kitchen table or island."

Laughs could be heard throughout the room.

"He's a good kid." I looked at Rylynn whose fork stopped midway up. She didn't catch my gaze. "He has some protective issues."

"Don't you all," Austyn threw in to more chuckles.

"Yeah. My girl is ten. She's livin' with me now. Long story, but her mom is wacked. She's in Girl Scouts, which I don't understand one bit, and likes to sing. Even if it is off key."

"Sounds like your sister," Princess threw in to Rylynn, who smiled.

"Yeah. They're very similar."

"Okay, so when can we ..." Ma started, but Pops interrupted by slapping a hand over her mouth. "Don't you dare. We talked about this shit. Knock it off."

Ma scowled at him, but judging from the happy faces around me, this was typical banter.

We ate and talked. Mostly light shit, not digging in too deep. I learned that Cooper and Bristyl were planning to elope to Vegas, which sent Austyn off the deep end. Nox and his woman were serious, but she'd been through some rough shit so she was gun-shy. Ryker and Austyn were good except for the bickering between them.

Princess and Cruz's relationship was one to watch. There was this push and pull between them that kept each of them on their toes. It was something I always wished my father could've had at some point in his life. He never had the woman at his side.

I admired each of them in their own ways.

It was a lot to take in. They were a lot to take in. It made me wonder what my life would've been like had I stayed with Cruz. But I shut that shit down fast because that was never an option, and I loved my dad. Thinking that way did nothing and solved nothing.

My cell rang, and I excused myself from the table answering it. "Crow."

"You get the girl?" Brewer teased.

"Was there any doubt?" I fired back.

He laughed. "What's the ETA for you comin' back?"

"Don't know. Why?"

Brewer started, "Damien wants a meet, and Ebony is due back soon." There was a shit load on my plate that needed to be worked out, and here I was having lunch with my new family while my old family was dealing with all the shit life was handing us.

"Give me tomorrow and I'll head back."

The phone was shuffled around on the other end. "You got it, boss. We'll have full updates for you when you arrive."

"Thanks."

He gave me a later, and I rung off. Turning around, Rylynn stood there. "Do you have to leave?" she asked, looking up at me. I pulled her into my body and wrapped my arms around her tight.

"Not yet. Need to give you time to pack your shit."

Her eyes narrowed. "First, I do not have shit." She paused. "Second, I don't know if I'm coming with you."

Pain sliced through me at the thought of her giving up on us. She couldn't. I wouldn't allow it. She felt for me what I did for her, and I'd never give up. My mind rolled with the possibilities of how to change her mind if it came to that. "Pixie."

She interrupted, "I know where you are, Crow.

When we get back to my place, I'll tell you where I am. We'll go from there."

I bent down and took her mouth. She reacted, kissing me back as her hands slipped through my hair. She wasn't going anywhere. Even if that meant strapping her to the back of my bike kicking and screaming.

CHAPTER EIGHTEEN
Rylynn

THE TALK. TRULY, I DIDN'T KNOW WHAT TO TELL CROW. Everything inside of me told me to give him another chance. To let him prove to me that he wasn't *that* man. That he was trustworthy. Fuck, that killed. I hated that we lost that. Hated that he didn't remember doing it.

Just hated it all.

We entered my place just as my cell rang. Looking at the display, it said *Mom calling*. It was like the heavens opened up giving me my mother. I took the call. "Hey, Mom."

"Hey there. Heard you went to the Cruz's house for brunch."

Ignoring what she said I replied, "Sure. I can come over. It'll be about thirty minutes though."

"What?" she asked.

"No problem. I can be there," I said out loud for Crow to hear.

"What is your deal? You swipe Grandma's pills?"

This made me want to chuckle, but I held it back. I needed to get to my mom's and have a talk. A real one. One that was down to the nitty-gritty of life.

"Okay, I'll see you in thirty." I didn't give her a chance to say anything because I hung up and turned to Crow. "I need to go to my mom's for a bit and help her with something. It won't take long."

"You want me to go with you?" he asked.

Fuck no. "My dad might be there, and I don't want to have to break you two up again."

"Keep thinkin' that, Pixie." He sat on the couch. "I'll be here when you get back."

"Great."

I grabbed my keys and without another word dashed to my Jeep, fired it up, and got the hell out of there. A bit down the road I dialed my mom who answered on the first ring with a "What the hell was that, Rylynn?"

"Mom, look. I need to talk to you alone. Are you home alone?"

"Are you okay?" She sounded concerned. It matched how I felt.

"Yes. Alone?"

"Will be for about an hour. Mazie is due back home

from Payton's house then. Why?" Looked like Mazie got her way after all.

"I'll be there in ten. Need to talk to you."

"Alright. Drive slow and get here safe."

I disconnected the line and drove to my mother's house.

Entering the house, my mom stood by the door worry all over her, from the hands twitching to the jaw jumping. "Mom, I'm fine. Just need to talk about Crow and me."

She let out an audible breath, pulled me into her arms, and kissed the top of my head. Mom led me over to the couch and we sat. "Talk," she ordered.

"Damn you sound like Dad, I retorted.

"Woman," she said sternly. This was one of those puzzles I didn't have the answer to, because feelings were involved. It wasn't a math problem that had a definite answer. There were so many variables involved, and it stumped me.

"Long story short..." I explained the time we had together. The reason for climbing on his bike. What happened at his house. What happened with Greer. What happened with Sophia. Then what happened last night. All of it. Every last detail, except the sex parts. She didn't need to have that seared on her brain. She was super cool and wouldn't care, but no thank you.

Mom leaned back in the couch, her gaze off in the

230 | RYAN MICHELE

distance. She was thinking. It was what she did every time something needed an answer that she didn't have at the tip of her tongue. I waited. And waited. Until she spoke.

"What is your heart saying?"

I answered immediately, "Go with him and see if we can make a go of it."

Her focus came to me. "Then that's what you do. Life doesn't give you a ton of chances. Sometimes it gives you none. This time it's holding its hand out and giving you something precious. Will it be work? Hell yes. You don't let that shit off the hook that easily. Crow does his time for it," she fired, and I smiled. There was my mom. "But you also don't hold it against him for long either if he shows you he can be who and what he tells you, then you let it go."

"And if I get hurt?"

Mom reached over and took my hand. "We always get hurt in one way or another. We hurt when we're in pain. We hurt when someone leaves us. We hurt when we stub our toe. We hurt when our best friend tells us we're fat."

My brows narrowed. "Fat?"

She waved her hand. "Just sayin' an example. But we all hurt. If you have him leave here with you knowing it'll be the last time you'll ever see him again, will that hurt?"

"Yeah," I whispered low.

"And you go with him and find out he's an asshole. Will that hurt?"

"Yeah, Mom."

"And if you go and things work out to where you're both happy, will that hurt?"

"No. I mean, it could."

She shook her head. "We don't live in a world where we make guesses on our future. We live it. Steer it in the direction we want and hope it stays on that track. I lost so many years without my dad. So many. If I could have a single one back, I would do it in a heartbeat. I just don't want you to regret something because that sticks with you forever."

I squeezed her hand knowing her pain at losing her dad and hating it for her at the same time. She was right. She always was.

"Not that I want you to leave though," she threw in there, making me laugh. "I mean, you have my grandbabies, you'd better be comin' home a lot."

My arms wrapped around my mom. "Not sure if that's going to happen any time soon."

"It will. One day." She pulled away and looked me straight in the eye. "You rely on your wisdom and heart, Rylynn. They will lead you in the right direction."

"Thanks, Mom."

"You're welcome. So what did you decide?"

Instead of answering, I smiled, kissed her, and took off.

But my Jeep didn't take me home. Instead, I drove around Sumner letting the wind whip through my hair. I should've stopped at the clubhouse and got my bike, but I didn't want to see anyone from there at the moment. I needed time.

The warmth caressed my skin as my mind rolled and milled. The roads passed by in a blur. Part of me wanted to tell Crow to take a long walk off a short pier. That what he did completely wiped the slate clean of our time together. While the other part wanted to hold onto him tight, and give him another chance to prove he was worth the risk. The thing was, I could only hold onto him if he let me. Crow was giving me that chance. The chance to hold on to him for the rest of our days.

He'd have a lot to atone for, but I'd be a complete moron if I let it slip through my fingers and not at least try. Like mom said, I'd regret it and wouldn't be able to turn back the clock. Living with the regret would be as bad as living with the reality what I wanted wasn't what it could be.

There was only one answer.

Fuck me.

"HEY," I called out, entering my apartment. Crow smiled from the couch, turning off the television and sitting up.

"Hey yourself. Get everything sorted?" he asked.

"Think so," I answered, tossing my keys to the table along with my bag and phone.

"So which way did your mom say to go?"

This made me smile. The man was too smart for his own damn good, knowing why I needed to go to my mother's. "You know, there can only be one Einstein in the family, and I've already claimed it."

"Nope, read it myself. There can be as many as you want."

I shook my head, moving to the couch and sitting on the opposite end of it. Reaching up, I pulled the hair tie out of my mass of hair and it fell around my shoulders. Running my hands through it, Crow watched the movements avidly. "We had a good talk."

He lifted his knee to the couch and turned fully to me give his full attention, which I liked. "Keep going."

A smile crept my lips. "You're not very patient, are you?"

He reached out and took my hand. "Pixie, when it comes to you I want everything."

This warmed me so much I could've melted. Why did I have to love this man so much? It would have been so much easier if he was a dick and turned a blind eye to me. Instead, he was kind and soft, something I knew he didn't show everyone else, yet I got it regularly.

Life. Love it or leave it. Since I didn't want to leave yet, I'd love it.

"You have to understand something, Crow. And this isn't some throwaway thing that you'll put in a box and it'll be lost forever."

"I get it," he responded, listening.

"This will be your only shot with me, Crow. You need to be all in because if I give you this, you have to know I won't stand for another woman touching you, kissing you, anything. I'll hurt them and then you. After that, I'm gone. There will be no more chances. There will be no words that could ever fix it. This is your one and only shot."

He stared at me for long moments. "Thank you," he shocked me saying.

"Huh?"

"I won't need another chance, Pixie. This is the only one I need, and I'll prove it down to my soul."

Fuck, he was going to make me cry.

He grasped me, pulled me to him, and kissed me hard.

Either my heart would be full or broken. Only time would tell.

CHAPTER NINETEEN
Crow

SHE COULDN'T COME UP FOR AIR BECAUSE I WOULDN'T let her. Devouring her mouth with everything I had inside of me, her hands wrapped around my neck and gave as good as she got. Picking her up by her ass, her legs wrapped around my hips as we continued kissing all the way to her bedroom.

I laid her down, coming with her as she fell. Pulling back, my hand brushed the side of her cheek. "You're it for me, Rylynn. Until I'm lyin' in a pine box, you're it."

Tears formed in her eyes, which wasn't like my strong Rylynn, but I'd admit, I liked it. It meant I was really getting through to her. I knew it would be an uphill battle, but fuck me I would hold on to her with everything I had.

Our lips joined once more, and we laid there

making out, taking our time, and just 'being' with each other in the moment.

Ever so slowly I pulled away and began to undress her. My fingertips glided up, catching her shirt and pulling. Her arms lifted as I tore the fabric from her body. Starting at her neck, I kissed and treasured every single inch of her as I went down.

Time was our friend, and my Pixie needed to know exactly how I felt about her. It wasn't enough to tell her; I needed to show her.

Goose bumps rose as her back arched into my touch. Moving up, I pulled the cups of her bra down one at a time making sure my finger ran across her nipple.

"You know," I started, all the while my fingers circled her now hardening peaks. They were beginning to turn red showing me how much this turned her on. "When I saw you the first time at the clubhouse, I wanted these tits." Hard, I pulled her flesh into my mouth sucking hard. She had beautiful breasts. "Having them once that night wasn't enough."

I blew cool air over her, her hands coming to my arms. "Crow."

A smile came across my face. "I'll never get enough of these. My cock sliding through them while I come all over your chest."

"Oh, God," she cried. Fuck, was she going to come

just from my words? This sounded like a challenge, which I was always up for.

"Oh yeah, Pixie. Then you'll clean my cock off with that sassy tongue of yours. Licking, sucking, and engulfing me so much I'll turn hard once again inside you."

Her nails dug into my shoulders. Even with my t-shirt on, there would be marks. I liked that idea a fuck of a lot. She started squirming in earnest, reaching down to try to unbutton her jeans.

Quickly, I grasped her wrists and held them above her head. "Not yet."

"Crow, I need you." Her words came out as breath, like she didn't have the control to talk. Loved how turned on this made her.

Popping her tit out of my mouth, our eyes connected. "You've got me. All of me. Only you." Entering her flesh back into my mouth, I was a hand down, but made do by rolling her other nipple between my fingers.

Rylynn was so jacked up that even with my weight on her she still tried to get friction between her legs. I switched breasts, continuing the torture.

"If you're all mine, give me your cock." This came out more stubborn. She was close and trying to hang on. One pinch of her nipple hard and her back arched off the bed taking me with it. She was right there. The cusp was upon us, and I wanted her to tumble over.

"You'll get it."

I released her wrists, pulled away from her tits, and took her mouth hard, my hands going to her breasts and squeezing them.

Rylynn exploded, ripping her lips from mine as she screamed out, her face a mask of pleasure as her neck bowed then came off the bed. "Crow. Fuck. Shit." She was making no sense as I continued to play with her nipples, having her ride it out.

It took a bite, but when her eyes opened they were astonished. "How'd you do that?"

My smile couldn't be hidden. "What, make you come so hard you saw fuckin' stars without even touchin' your pussy."

"Cocky."

The smile grew. "Fuck, Pixie. You're damn beautiful."

My plan was to make love to her, but with what she just gave me, my cock was hard as a rock and needed to be buried deep in her pussy. After one more kiss, I lifted and tore her jeans and underwear from her body, getting her shoes off as I went.

After divesting of my clothes, I gave her no preamble. My cock went through her wet folds with ease taking me all the way to the root.

"Get ready," I warned her, getting up on my knees and holding her legs spread apart. Using everything inside of me, I thrust in and out of her, over and over again. Her eyes rolled in the back of her head at one point, but I didn't relent.

"Fuck me hard, Crow," she said, only spurring me on. She wasn't the only one who got off on the talk.

Hand to her clit, I rubbed hard as she screamed out, and I came inside my woman.

Mine.

All fucking mine.

Forever.

"You said you were all in," I reminded Rylynn as I brushed the hair away from her beautiful face.

"Yeah," she answered, eyes showing me just how much she wanted this. Fucking loved that.

"Gotta head back. You comin'?"

She shook her head. "No."

My heart stopped, and air wouldn't come in my lungs. No. She was bailing? "No?" I asked.

She smiled, but I wasn't feeling it. "I have things that need to be closed up here, Crow. This is more than me hopping on your bike and driving away with you. I need to go through all my stuff, pack what I need, store what I don't. I also need to close up the cases I'm on and let Naddy know."

"Naddy?"

"She helps me with getting clients. She'll need to know my location change, and somehow I'll need to get feelers out for Alabama."

"You don't need to work."

She quirked her brow, and her hand went to hip. "I have to work, Crow. Not only do I love what I do, I'm not some mooch who lives off someone. That isn't me."

"I know that's not you, Rylynn. Just sayin' until you get on your feet, you don't have to worry."

"I will, Crow. Coming with you does not mean you support me."

That didn't sit right with me. "You're my woman. Yes, I take care of what is mine. That means I take care of you. You want to work, that's up to you, but, Pixie, make no mistake—I take care of you."

"We'll cover that another time."

She smiled mischievously. Inside I did too because Rylynn in any way made my dick hard. I had a feeling that I'd be hard for the rest of my damn life with her in it. Fuck yeah, I'd like that.

"Anyway." She cut into my thoughts. "I'll come, but I need to get things ready. It will take a few days."

"Days?"

"You think it's easy packing up a life to make a new one?"

I shook my head. "No, Pixie, just don't want to be without you." She melted into me, her head resting on my chest, my arms around her tight. Yeah. Even missing this a day sucked.

"See what I mean about you being sweet."

"You can't tell anyone. It'll ruin me."

She laughed hard, a sound I loved hearing. Truly, I didn't give a fuck about that shit. I was who I was. Blood on my hands and all.

"We have something to do before you leave."

This had my cock hardening once again. "We are so doing that."

She smiled and shook her head. "No. We need to go to my parents. We need to tell them what's happening, and I need to tell my sister."

"You know she's going to kick me or something," I teased, but was serious. That little girl had a strong grip on who she was.

"Yeah. She will, but we need to."

Kissing the top of her head, I replied, "Yeah. We do."

"I'll call and get everyone rounded up."

THREE HOURS LATER, I was pulling into Rylynn's childhood home with a pissed off Rhys standing on the porch, arms crossed waiting for us. His glare was tight and brows knitted.

Rylynn climbed off behind me as I shut the bike down, put out the stand, and swung off.

"This is gonna go well," I said into her hair.

She smiled. "You want this, this is part of the price."

"Smartass."

Wrapping my arm around her shoulders, I pulled her in close to me and kissed her temple. Whatever this visit became, I'd know where I stood with Rhys. Hopefully, it wouldn't be six feet under. There was no doubt he had a gun on him. I did too for that matter, but shooting him wasn't in the plan.

Rylynn pulled away from me and wrapped her arms around her father. I heard her whisper, "Don't kill him, Daddy. I love him."

Fuck, that felt good.

"We'll see," Rhys said, kissing the top of her head. "Your mother needs you inside for a minute."

Rylynn's eyes went back and forth between us, indecision plaguing her. She knew what was about to go down. She had no control, something my woman didn't like. She was in the middle of the two men she loved. Hated that for her, but understood it all the same. "Pixie, it's good. Go help your mom."

"You'd better not be bloody when I come back out here," she said, glaring at us and storming off into the house. Fire. Loved it.

"Make no promises," Rhys said as she shut the door.

Such was life, this could go many ways. I was ready for all of them. He hated me and I got that, but it wouldn't solve anything. If he needed to throw his fists again, we'd do it and end up bloody with Rylynn kicking both our asses. Not the route I'd choose to take, but one I wouldn't back down from either.

"So you're still around," Rhys said, pressing his back against the house while I stood by the railing of the porch.

"Looks like it."

He scoffed, "She deserves better."

"Know that. Doesn't mean I'm gonna give her up." She deserved so much better than me. I knew it down to my soul. Didn't mean a damn thing though. She was mine.

"So that means you're takin' my girl to Alabama?" he questioned, not looking at me but out at the quiet road, appearing lost in thought.

"Yeah."

He shook his head. "I want to rip your fuckin' heart out and burn it," Rhys said. "It's takin' everything inside of me not to beat your ass to a pulp for fuckin' over my girl."

"We already did that part. Remember?"

"Like I could forget." He stood like a statue, not giving anything away. But whatever it was, he just needed to get on with it. There was shit to do and if he needed to beat my ass again, then let's do it. That's what men did. We fought, got it out, and moved the fuck on. With Rhys though, one never knew what would come out of his mouth or fists.

"I have a daughter and if any motherfucker did to them what I did to Rylynn, they'd be dead. Get it. The fact I'm not six feet under is a miracle. She wants to see where this goes. I've told her where it's gonna go. My ring on her finger and babies in her belly. She needs to trust me again. I get that, and I'll bust my ass for it."

"Good luck with that," he said.

"Believe me. I know I have my work cut out for me."

He stepped away from the house and turned to me. "Why the fuck did you do it?"

My head shook. "Still don't fuckin' know. Keep replayin' that shit over and over in my head, but there's blank spots in my memories. I obviously did it so there are no excuses to be made. It's my cross to bear and will do it."

"You don't remember? Seriously, man." He didn't believe me. Fuck, *I* didn't believe myself. I'd done everything in my life to the letter knowing this patch would be on my back and the responsibility that came with it. For me to do something so damn stupid was unusual. But there were no answers that I could give him.

Fuck, I hated this shit.

"Know you don't believe it. That shit isn't a throwaway though. It's the honest to God truth, swear it on my fuckin' cut, but it doesn't change the fact that I hurt Rylynn. That shit won't happen again."

His gaze swept over me, no doubt reading whatever he could from my posture and facial expressions. The man had always been good at it. It was one of his specialties. I was telling him the truth so I didn't give a fuck. He could look all he wanted and if he saw something he didn't like, that was on him, not me.

"She's fuckin' half your age," he said out of the blue.

"And you're older than her mom. The point is?"

He smirked. Actually fucking smirked. Fuck. Hadn't seen him do that in a while. "The point is she's young and has a lot going for her in this life. Doesn't need someone tying her down and not letting her soar."

"She's an old soul, but you know that. Smart as hell and a great head on her shoulders. She knows this life. Loves it. Lives it. And, brother, she can fly as high as she wants and I'll be by her thick and thin."

His head tipped back, his hands going into his hair, then down his face. "Fuck, it's history repeating itself."

Remembering what Ry told me about her parents, I responded, "All of it but the fuckin' up part. From what Rylynn says, you didn't have that step."

He shrugged. "We all fuck up. Just depends on the depth of it."

"True. Very true."

He came to stand shoulder to shoulder with me, and I didn't budge. "You know that if you hurt her again, they won't be able to identify your body."

It was my turn to laugh. "Know it. I won't. But if something ungodly happens and I do, you need to cut me up because I wouldn't be able to live with myself."

His hand came to my shoulder squeezing it tight. "That's the shit a dad wants to hear."

My head shook. "Is our heart to heart over? I have a mom and sister to win over."

He chuckled deep. "You thought I was hard. Mazie'll rip you to shreds."

That I had no doubt.

Entering the house first, I was met with a ten-year-old ball of fury. Mazie stomped up to me. It was cute in her light pink ruffled dress that didn't match her personality one bit. Her blonde hair was up in pigtails and curly on the ends. Yeah. Cute, but not. The snake underneath her bit hard.

"Did you hurt my daddy?" Hands on her hips she sneered, looking all the way up at me with not one ounce of fear. Kid had balls. Hopefully, she knew when to use them and when to not. Not all men were me.

Rhys walked in. "He didn't hurt me the first time, Maz."

"He made you bleed," she retorted, still giving me

the evil eye, and it was a damn good one she must've worked hard on.

"I made him bleed worse," Rhys added.

"Right," I jumped in.

Rhys nodded down to his daughter. "You do want to leave here with your balls, right?"

This made me laugh, but Mazie didn't find anything funny as she glared up at me. "As you can see, your dad is just fine."

"He'd better be," she said just as Rylynn walked into the living room, a dish towel in her hand.

"Seriously," Rylynn barked at her parents. "You're gonna let her talk like that? She's gonna be that little shit in school everyone's afraid of so she doesn't have any friends."

"I have friends!" Mazie yelled.

"One, Payton. If you were nicer and not such a brat, others would want to be your friend."

"Alright, enough." Rhys stepped in between his daughters. "Mazie, your sister's right. Love that you have spark, but you gotta learn when to tone it down."

Mazie's mouth dropped open as she stared at her dad. No, he'd never said those things to her before, and she was utterly stunned. She couldn't even move the shock was so much.

"It's all about control, Mazie. Gotta know when to put your emotions in check and when to let them out.

One of these times, you're gonna mess with someone bigger than you and it won't be pretty."

"But you'll beat 'em up for me," she said knowingly.

"You know I protect you but, Maz, sometimes it's too late and you need to know how to protect yourself."

"Finally," Rylynn said, coming up to my side, my arm going around her shoulders. "You gotta chill, monkey. Know you were pissed at Crow, but that's over now and we're movin' on."

"What does that mean?" Mazie asked.

Rylynn released me and bent down to her sister. "It means that I'm movin' to Alabama to be with Crow."

"What?" Mazie's eyes got as big as saucers as her little frame went even tighter, if that was possible.

Rylynn reached out for her sister, who stated statue still. "In a couple of days, I'm gonna move to Alabama. I'll come and visit just like I do now, and you can come and see me too."

"But Alabama is a whole state away." Tears brimmed her eyes. "You can't leave."

Rylynn's hand went through Mazie's curly cue of hair pulling it in front of her face. "I have to. It's time for me."

"It's not. It's because of him!" she screamed it as a curse.

Rylynn didn't take her shit. Instead, she gripped onto Mazie's arms forcing her to look her in the face. "Monkey," she called out, and Mazie fought it, but at the name she had to look. "One day, when you love someone, you'll want to move to be with him too. It's part of life. We grow and learn new things."

"I'm never loving anyone but my daddy."

"Right," Rylynn said, looking up at me. Fuck, my daughter didn't talk to me like Mazie did. I was no help there so I shrugged. "Look, Maz. We have the phone and video chat. We can talk all the time."

The little girl deflated, all the bravado sweeping out of her like a balloon as she collapsed in Rylynn's arms sobbing. Rylynn had a few tears of her own, but hid them well.

She would miss her family, and I'd need to make the transition was as smooth as possible for her so she could stay connected to her family.

"I've gotta go."

Brewer called earlier this morning saying that the meet with Damien was scheduled for later tomorrow and they had information on the Purple Pride. All shit that needed to be dealt with. Therefore, I had to go.

Didn't like leaving my woman here, but it was what needed to be done for her to come to me. She needed to close up shop, and I needed to get shit as taken care of as possible by the time Rylynn showed up.

I pulled her in my arms. "Two days, right?"

She nodded. "I'll do my best, but can't say that it's written in stone."

"Make it be."

She smiled. "I'll miss you too, Grizzly."

That had me smiling. It had been a while since she called me that. "Thought you forgot about that."

Her fingers went into my hair and pulled it slightly at the nape. "Never."

Our lips collided as I tasted her, breathing her in like air. Breathless, she pulled away. "I'll be there soon. Okay?"

"Yeah." I bent down and kissed her once more. If I didn't get out now, I'd be stuck here because no way in fuck I wanted to leave her. As I drove away from Sumner, a huge chunk of me didn't come, and I felt that down to my bones.

CHAPTER TWENTY
Crow

Brewer met me on the way into the clubhouse, slapping me on the shoulder. "How'd that go?" he asked, knowing where I went. I'd called him before hopping on my bike and heading out to Sumner. It didn't take a rocket scientist to know what was the goal of this visit.

"She'll be here in a couple of days."

We started walking going through the door and inside. "Looks like she got in a few good punches on ya."

"Rhys."

Brewer stopped. "Fuck, good?"

I reached around the bar and grabbed a beer, flipping the top off, the sound clattering to the bar top. "We both needed it." Looking around the clubhouse, a few women milled around along with a few of the guys. "Office."

We moved, Brewer on my heels as we went down the stairs and shut the door to my office. Rounding the desk, I sat my ass in the chair and Brewer sat in front of me, legs stretched out comfortably.

"The night of my old man's funeral. Did you see me kiss Sophia?"

He nodded. "Yep. Did it right in front of the club."

"Was something off with me?" I asked, rubbing my hands over my face. This situation was bothering me more than I cared to admit, but it was there nagging in the back of my head.

"Other than shocking the shit out of me considering Rhys was there. Thought maybe you had a death wish," he replied.

"Brother, I don't remember that shit. Somethin's not right."

Brewer sat up putting his elbows to his knees. "What are you thinkin'?"

My head shook. "Not sure, but I'm gonna have Wrong Way look through the feeds of the club to see if anything was off."

"Let me know what I can do." He leaned back. "Whatever it was, since she's comin' here, it's good?"

"It will be."

"Now who's the one doing the counseling," Brewer teased, and I shot him a glare that was anything but.

"Enough of that shit. What's goin' on?"

It was time to get down to business and get some of this shit off my plate.

Brewer started in, "Damien is meetin' us at the Warf at seven tomorrow night." The Warf was a local bar that was a hole in the wall, but the people running it were our kind of people. Therefore, the location worked in our favor.

"Sounds good. How'd he sound?"

"What do ya mean?"

I continued, "Jittery? Confident? Strung out?"

"Just like any other asshole trying to take something that wasn't his in the first place." That I could accept.

"You said you had info on The Pride," I said, moving us along.

Brewer sat up in his chair. "First, Simon is pissed as shit he was moved out of Sophia's place."

"He givin' her shit?"

"Ethan had to physically remove him from the property. He's going to be a problem that will need to take care of."

Placing my arms on my desk and leaning forward, I responded, "That would give me great pleasure to do." It also made me feel good that even though Sophia was pissed at me, she knew I'd never put her or my boy in danger. She listened.

"Figured as much." He paused. "She hasn't let him

254 | RYAN MICHELE

in, so whatever you said got through to her." Confirmation. Liked that.

"Good."

"Those two in the back of the pack, the sweaty and jittery."

"I remember them, Brewer."

"Right." He reached in his cut and pulled out a stack of papers that he handed to me, and I started looking through. "We got the drop on them."

In my hand were pictures of the two assholes, addresses, phone numbers and their rap sheets, which didn't give me much, but the kicker was one named Barry Alabaster. Dark brown hair, brown eyes, and a somewhat pudgy face. "You're shittin' me."

Brewer shook his head. "Nope. For a man who likes to beat women, he appears to be a pussy. And he changed his hair dark from the pictures found at his house."

"Men who beat women are pussies. He's goin' full off radar. Fucker."

"True. The problem is Barry is still invisible. No word on the money from the safe. The other guy, Rodney Burman, we haven't had time to scope out."

"Scope it and then put Jimmy on it so we can get the fuckers."

Brewer nodded, but didn't reach for his phone. "Ebony's men say she's due back by the end of the week."

"Hopefully we know what we're dealin' with before then."

"Right." He lifted his phone. "I'll get calls out."

"Guns?"

"We're meetin' Wells not tomorrow but the next night. He's got the cash, and we'll do the swap. Any decision on Starling?"

"No. It's not changin', so don't ask me again."

He knocked on my desk once. "Right. I'll get on this."

"Get the guys to make sure the load is taken care of."

"Already done."

"Good."

WITH A LITTLE TIME TO SPARE, I took a drive by Jenny's old house to see if she happened to be around. While it was true, I was done with her, there was hope she'd pull her head out of her ass and get clean for her kid.

Unfortunately, it was a small hope, but it was there nonetheless. She wasn't there. The house empty.

Riding around Rebellion, I gave low waves to those I knew or chin lifts. This was my town. Mine to protect. Mine to look out for. Mine to take care of.

Phoenix and Tex met up with me flanking my sides

as we continued our ride through. Home. One that I was going to make damn sure Rylynn felt good in.

On the outskirts of town, a small eatery lay that was the hidden gem of Rebellion. The Corner Square was a mom and pop shop, been here since before I was born. Food was fabulous. It reminded me I needed to bring Rylynn here.

The door to the shop opened, and two men exited. The two men who were at the football game that called us a gang saying the Panthers sucked. I stuck out my hand getting my brothers attention as the two men began to walk into the parking lot.

Sticking out my hand, my brothers followed me into the parking lot. We pulled up and parked, the two men oblivious to their surroundings. Another one of their many mistakes.

We swung off our bikes, Phoenix and Tex coming up beside me. "Fuckers from the football game."

Phoenix maniacally grinned, while Tex cracked his knuckles.

Blocking the men's paths, they jolted.

"What the..." the stubby one said then hit his friend stick's arm. "Those are the ..." Fear flashed in both of their eyes. Good.

"See you remember us," I said as Phoenix and Tex charged them, grabbing them around the neck and marching them behind The Corner Square. The assholes feet dragged, and hands needed to be clamped around their mouths to shut them up.

Luckily, we were able to get them behind the building before they caught attention.

"Seems you missed our message the first time," I growled. "You're not welcome in Rebellion."

At the same time, both Tex and Phoenix punched the asshole they held in the gut. They fell to the ground.

I stepped up closer. "This will be a reminder and your only one."

The three of us descended on them, fists flying and legs kicking. Their cries were muffled with bone-crushing punches in the jaw.

I let the frustration of my life pour out of me, releasing it on these two dicks.

They moaned on the ground as we stepped back. "Stay the fuck out of Rebellion." On a spit down at them, we walked away.

You didn't fuck with Rebellion or the Ravage MC.

CHAPTER TWENTY-ONE
Rylynn

"I CAN'T BELIEVE YOU'RE LEAVING," AUSTYN SAID, wrapping her arms around me tight. Yeah, I'd miss her like crazy. "Not only that, you're going to live with my brother. How weird is that?"

"It is strange I guess."

She pulled away. "I'm actually jealous you get to go there. I feel like I don't even know him, and we have the same dad. Here you are going to him."

"Don't be throwin' that green-eyed monster my way." I gave a smile trying to break her mood. It didn't work. "You can come and see us, and I'll be sure to bring him here."

"Promise," Austyn demanded.

"Promise."

She hugged me once again, and that was when the Ravage MC descended on me. Coming at me from different angles. Some happy for me. Others threat-ening to murder Crow if he hurt a hair on my toe. But all of them missing me before I had even left.

This was family. My family.

I couldn't say I wasn't nervous because part of me was. Starting an entirely new life wasn't easy. New friends, clients, job, man, club—all of it wrapped up together as a monumental change. Hopefully a year from now it wouldn't feel so tedious to climb. I would just be celebrating having made it to the top.

Nox was one of the last ones to come up to me in the clubhouse. I loved Nox like a brother. He had my back during the in-between phase of my grandfather's death. He even gave me closure letting me know his death was avenged. He'd been there for me in a way no one else had and fuck, I was gonna miss him.

"Really packin' up and leavin' the good life?" he questioned, taking a pull on his beer.

"Looks like it."

He turned fully to me getting in my space. There-fore, I had to look up at him. "You need any-fuckin-thing, I'm only a phone call away," he said, wrapping his arms around me and pulling me deep into him. He let go and walked away.

Yeah, that one hurt. So much so, I needed the bath-room so I wouldn't break down.

My Jeep was packed with the things I needed while other stuff was staying in a storage unit that

Ravage owned. My apartment would be put up for rent once again and that was that. I was really putting one foot in front of the other and moving on with my life.

Never thought that move would be away from one Ravage MC and into another. Same, but different. Life had a funny way of showing itself sometimes.

But it was time to start anew. Crow and I had a hill to climb, but I had faith he'd show me there was nothing to worry about. It would take time, but like I told him, I was all in for the ride.

The last three goodbyes were going to be the worst, and I avoided my parents and Mazie like the plague. Not wanting to do it, yet knowing I had to. It wasn't a goodbye forever. Rather a see you later.

They weren't that far away, and I could make it here in a few hours if I was needed. The thing was, I'd never lived away from home. Away from my folks, at least like this. It was a huge step for me, and no doubt a huge step for them as well.

They weren't losing me, but it might feel that way to them. It was time though. Time to get them away from the crowd. It was one of the few times that I was fully nervous, but that was because this was going to hurt in a way that I'd leave marks deep inside. I hated it, but understood it at the same time.

Walking into the kitchen area of the club, my mom was talking to Angel, GT's ol' lady. When I approached,

Angel gave me a knowing smile, hugged me, and left us alone.

"You're really goin'?" my mom asked, but it really came out as a confirmation of fact.

"Yeah."

She smiled. "I should've told ya he was no good and not to listen to your heart. That he was a dumb-fuck who didn't deserve to breathe your air."

A chuckle escaped. "Yeah, you probably should."

She pulled me into her arms and wrapped me up tight. "I'm so proud of you, Rylynn. The woman you've become. It's damn admirable how you've built your business and did it all on your own. Know starting new in Rebellion you'll take a hit with that but, baby girl, swear to you, I know you'll make it work."

Her arms pushed me back as she stared into my eyes, hers glistening with tears. "You have always had a good head planted on your shoulders. Don't ever lose that. Life is bumpy. So many twists and turns, but once you reach the other side, it's a beauty you'll never regret."

Tears spilled down my face. There was no use in even trying to hold them back, because it wasn't happening. Loved my mom with everything inside of me. And I'd miss her like crazy.

"What if this decision is fucked up? What if I learn it's not where I want to be?"

She smiled warmly. "Then you can always come

back to Sumner. We aren't goin' anywhere, but don't go into this as Sumner bein' your way out. You only go into this if you feel in your heart and soul it's the right move for you."

My throat caught, and I had to clear it. "It is. It's the right move."

Mom squeezed my arms, giving me a broken smile. I felt her sadness of me leaving, but she was right.

"Then you go and build your life, Rylynn."

"Love you."

Tears fell from her eyes matching my own as she pulled me into a tight hug. "Love you. Always and forever, my girl."

She held me for long moments, before pulling away. "You talk to your father yet?"

"No. Figured I'd talk to Mazie first, then tackle Dad."

"He's havin' a hard time with this, Ry. You're his baby, no matter the age."

This choked me up again. "Yeah."

Mom gave me a smile, then another hug. After wiping my face, I searched for my sister who was outside the clubhouse. Booker, Breaker and Shaina's kid, was there looking down at Mazie and sneering. Lord only knew what those two were up to.

The way she didn't back down and the way he was confident even at thirteen-years-old. It was going to be a match made in hell. Those two always fought. Mazie was young and didn't see it the way I did. Booker would move heaven and earth for her, and she had no clue. Hell, he probably had no clue.

That was something I'd miss watching play out over the years.

Putting my fingers between my lips, a high-pitched whistle caught my sister's attention. Her head swung around, saw me, and she ran full on colliding with my legs. Her head came up to my stomach now, and she for sure would be as tall as me one day. We hugged for a bit, until she looked up at me and said, "You're going now."

She was so damn smart. I hoped she got a handle on the brat side. She had so much to give the world, if she did what our father said and learned to control it.

I grabbed her hand and led her out to the picnic table, hopping up on it, she followed. "Yeah, monkey."

Mazie started crying, and I wrapped her in my arms. "I'll be back to visit a lot. Remember about the texting and video chats? We have that."

"Gonna miss you," she said, laying her head on my chest as her body shook.

"I'll miss you too but, Mazie, this is just a change in location. I'm still here." I tapped her chest.

"Grandpa is there too."

This choked me up because in all of this, the ups and downs of what had happened, I hadn't put those two things together. It made me feel like shit. "Yeah, always. But I'm not dead, Maz. I'm just livin' some-where else. Gotta know there's a huge difference in that."

"It sucks."

I kissed the top of her head. "Yeah. It does."

"You don't get to stop being my sister," she added in.

This made me smile. "Never."

We sat there until her tears subsided and only got up when a car came through the gates of the club-house. I knew instantly who it was and took off to it, Mazie on my heels. The passenger side door swung open, and my breath caught.

"Grandma." I moved to her as she gave me a small smile. She was doing better, but still a bit weak. Her strength just hadn't returned to normal. The hang around from the other night got out of the car, asked if we needed help, and took off.

I helped her out of the car and Mazie went to wrap her arms around her, but I grabbed her arm stopping her. Mazie could be a bit rough.

"Let's go over there," Grandma, also known as Mearna, said, nodding at the lawn chairs over by the fire. She could walk but was fragile, and I hated that.

After getting her set down, Mazie started chat-tering on, and Grandma let her get it all out. This took a long time, but when Mazie finally hopped off, Grand-ma's full attention was on me.

"Just because I'm not my full self doesn't mean you get to leave Sumner without talkin' to me, young lady." I made to speak, but she held up her hand. "Talkin' to me is not going to make me sicker."

That wasn't entirely true since the doctors said that the stress of my grandpa's death didn't help with her recovery, and anything could make it veer in the wrong direction. It wasn't that I didn't want to spend time with her. I just didn't want to hurt her more.

"Sorry, Gram."

There were no excuses for avoiding her except stupidity. I didn't need to lose both grandparents. Shit.

"Now, your mother tells me you met a man and are movin' to Alabama," she started, then recited pretty much the entire story I'd given my mother the other day. No surprise there. They were tight.

"Yeah. I'm goin'," I answered as she reached over and grabbed my hand. It looked so frail compared to mine. Not the grandma I'd known for nineteen years. I hated that for her.

"When I met your grandfather, he was it for me. Loved that man more than my next breath." She shook her head, looking around the club. "One time and that was it for me. He was it for me."

"Know that, Gram."

She gave a sad smile. "I lied."

This shocked the shit out of me, and my body tensed. "What?"

"Stupid. I was young and dumb, never knowing what I wanted to do with my life. Met this man in a biker bar and fell head over heels." She looked my way. "But, Ry, I didn't just leave because I didn't want your momma to grow up here," I said nothing, waiting. "Your grandpa was a ladies' man. From the moment I met him, I knew this for fact considering he had three women pawing at him for his attention."

This didn't surprise me one bit.

"I'm not gettin' where you lied, Gram."

She stared off into the distance. "At the time, I wasn't strong enough to hack seeing the women all over him. It drove me mad, but I was a girl from a small town just tryin' to make my way in life. When I ended up pregnant, I left. It wasn't the MC lifestyle, but it was. It was my insecurities of not being enough for him. The women around him were beautiful, and here I was pregnant with his child. He wouldn't want me for long. So I left."

My heart squeezed for her.

"Gram, you're beautiful. He said he loved you from the very beginning."

Her smile widened. "Yes, I know that now, but I didn't know that then. I let my fears hold me back and missed out on so many years with that man."

"What are you tryin' to tell me here?"

Her legs twisted so her knees were now touching mine. Connected. "Life is a big puzzle." This made me smile, her knowing my love for them. "Each action you take has a reaction somewhere down the line. For me, my action was leaving Dagger. The reaction was missing more than twenty years with him and causing my daughter to grow up without a father. It was a reaction that I brought on myself, yet killed me at the same time." She paused, letting that hang before she continued.

"Just like Crow. You say he kissed another woman, that was his action. Your reaction was to leave." Her hands shook just a bit in mine, but she kept firing away. "You didn't cause him to kiss her, but yet you left him because of it."

"He says he doesn't remember, Gram." At those words, a cool breeze came across the yard dimming the heat of the sun. "What do I do with that?"

"The trust has been broken. The only way to fix it is to work together to rebuild it. He may not remember. That is something you need to work out. The bottom line is that you love him."

I nodded in agreement.

"Love has a way of working things out in the end. I found my way back to your grandpa after years of being apart. I'd never stopped loving him. You can overcome anything if both people in the relationship are on the same page."

"Gram. I believe him. I know I probably shouldn't.

But in my gut, I do. It's just the why he doesn't remember part that bothers me."

She shook my hand. "Another puzzle to solve."

"Not sure about this one."

Mazie jogged up with two glasses. "Mom said to give you these. It's sweet tea." We took them, and she trotted off.

"Your mother always knows when I need something."

I took a drink. "She's a smart woman."

"You are too. Always remember that. I may have started out not sure of myself, but I learned. I taught your mother to be strong, and she taught you. Three generations of strength to get you through all of life's ups and downs."

It was amazing when she put it like that. It was empowering.

"Do you think I've lost my mind moving to be with a man?"

She shook her head. "Not for a second. If I knew then what I know now, I'd have moved to Antarctica to be with your grandfather. Everyone is different. There is no cookie cutter, must do this or must do that list. You have to figure out how you work together."

"Anyone ever tell you, you were smart? But you can't have Einstein, that's me."

Gram chuckled. "Einstein huh? That's a new one."

"Not really. After all, I do come from a damn good gene pool."

We laughed together, reminding me of the times before my grandpa passed away. There was laughter now, but it was always missing his gruff tone.

"Yes, you do. Now you go on and give them hell over there. Let them know what a Ravage woman is made of."

"Yes, ma'am."

She handed me her drink which I set down in the grass. "I need to go inside where it's cool. The heat is givin' me a bit of a headache."

Without a moment of delay, I helped her up and into the clubhouse. Leaning down, I kissed her cheek. "Love you."

"Love you too."

Nox came up beside me and handed me a beer. I took it with pleasure. "Thanks."

"Know you're drivin' so only one, but you may need it for your chat with your dad."

Looking over my shoulder, my father sat at the table, beer in hand but his gaze far off in the distance. Knowing I had a long drive ahead, I set the beer down saying, "Thanks, Nox" and took off to talk to my father.

Pulling up a chair, I sat next to him. He didn't miss a beat. "Not fuckin' tellin' you bye."

My hand went to his that was holding the bottle of

beer like a vice grip. "No. You'll tell me, see ya later. Because I'm comin' back, Dad."

"Not to stay though."

Fuck, why did shit like this have to be so hard? "I love you."

"Love you too." He leaned over and kissed the top of my head. "You be safe drivin'. You get in any trouble you call me. And if that fucker hurts you again, I'll cut his balls off."

"Don't worry, Daddy. I told him the same thing."

Only then did I get a small smile from him. He'd always been a man of few words, but this was completely different. I hated that I was the one who put that lost look on his face. Moving into him, I wrapped him up in my arms, him doing the same.

"Proud of the woman you've become, Rylynn. Always know that."

That was when the tears started to fall from my face in steady streams. We didn't move from that position until I was able to compose myself. I sure as hell didn't know how much a person could cry, but I'd met my quota for the decade.

"Get outta here," my father said. Giving him a soft smile, hugs to everyone once again, I climbed in my Jeep and took off.

Destination: Rebellion, Alabama.

THE DRIVE WAS peaceful and gave me time to think, reflect on my choices and decisions. In my gut, I knew this was the right decision, being with Crow. Was I still hurt by what I saw? Yes. That feeling wouldn't go away for a while I'd supposed. Under that though was more. We had such a solid foundation, and then the earthquake came and shook the place.

I wanted to get back to being solid, knowing Crow was mine and only mine.

Was there a bit of fear this could all blow up in my face. Yes. It was there in the background just waiting for its chance to come alive. But I was a Hutton, and we didn't let fear hold us back. We were strong and determined.

That was what I was going to be.

When I called Crow about an hour ago to tell him I was an hour out, he was out on club business and told me where his extra key was. He said I was to stay in his house until he got there. He was going to have to learn, he didn't dictate what I did or when.

I was not a woman to be barked orders at, but he already knew it. He always wanted to rile me up, and I let him freely. Loved having that back and forth with him.

It was something I never wanted to disappear.

Since I really didn't know anyone here, staying at his place wouldn't be a hardship.

Pulling up to his house, this time I wasn't in awe of it. No, this time I felt like I was home. My apartment never felt that way, but my parents' house did. Now, with Crow's home, I felt it the instant my Jeep hit the driveway.

Yeah, this was the right decision.

I parked in the driveway and grabbed my bag. I had to pee like a racehorse, then I'd unload the boxes from my Jeep. Crow would be pissed that I didn't wait for him, but he'd get over it because all the boxes would already be in the place by the time he got here.

Making my way up the walk, I reached down to a small rock that was barely noticeable. Picking it up, I pulled out the key from its mystery hiding spot. I did this smiling. Yes, this was a great start to a fantastic life for Crow and me. Happy. That was what we needed.

Shoving the key in the lock, the door flew open.

Everything around me stopped.

Breaths ceased.

Time stood still.

Feet wanted to float instead of staying put.

Nothing felt right.

Everything hurt.

Once again.

Because standing in Crow's door was Sophia.

Oops, I did it again. No that wasn't the cheesy line from Britney Spears. Okay, so it was. This 'book' needed to be broken up into three separate books. There was so much going on, and once again I couldn't condense. BUT! I promise you, there will only be three books. NO MORE.

Sealed in Strength is coming very soon.

Thank you for reading, and I hope you loved Crow and Rylynn as much as I did.

~Ryan

ACKNOWLEDGEMENTS

Editing by: Silla Webb at Masque of the Red Pen

Cover Design by: Cassy Roop at Pink Ink Designs

Photography by: Wander Aguiar at Wander Aguilar Photography

Models: Nathan Van Dyken

ABOUT RYAN

Ryan Michele found her passion in bringing fictional characters to life. She loves being in an imaginary world where anything is possible, and she has a knack for special twists readers don't see coming.

She writes MC, Contemporary, Erotic, Paranormal, New Adult, Inspirational, and other romance-based genres. Whether it's bikers, wolf-shifters, mafia, etc., Ryan spends her time making sure her heroes are strong and her heroines match them at every turn.

When she isn't writing, Ryan is a mom and wife, living in rural Illinois and reading by her pond in the warm sun.

Join my Reader Group: https://www.facebook.com/groups/RyansSultrySinners/

Sign Up for my newsletter: https://www.subscribepage.com/918BackmatterSignUps

Come find me:
www.authorryanmichele.com
ryanmicheleauthor@gmail.com

facebook.com/authorryanmichele

twitter.com/Ryan_Michele

instagram.com/author_ryan_michele

bookbub.com/authors/ryan-michele

Thank you for reading!